'I am choosi... mistress to the Sheikh.

He made it sound so...*mechanical.* 'Is there a new vacancy, then?' Sienna questioned acidly. 'Or will I be sharing the post?'

Hashim was so used to complete compliance—to grateful and eager acceptance from adoring women—that for a moment he was taken aback by her flippant attitude. 'I do not think you realise the honour I am affording you,' he said icily.

'No, I probably don't,' said Sienna gravely. 'Perhaps you could tell me a little more about what this exciting position entails?'

'You will have an open charge account.' His black eyes flicked disparagingly over her jeans and stained T-shirt. 'And in future you will buy clothes that please you, and please your Sheikh. I should like to see you in silks and satins from now on.'

'How delightfully simple you make it sound,' Sienna murmured. 'Anything else?'

EXPOSED: THE SHEIKH'S MISTRESS

BY
SHARON KENDRICK

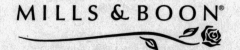

With special thanks to Paul McLaughlin, editor of
Kroll's Report On Fraud—and a pretty mean writer himself!

*First published in Great Britain 2005
Harlequin Mills & Boon Limited,
Eton House, 18-24 Paradise Road, Richmond, Surrey TW9 1SR*

© Sharon Kendrick 2005

ISBN 0 263 84176 6

*Set in Times Roman 10½ on 13 pt.
01-0905-40996*

*Printed and bound in Spain
by Litografia Rosés, S.A., Barcelona*

CHAPTER ONE

IF ONLY there had been some kind of warning…storm clouds gathering on the horizon, perhaps, or a sudden chill wind which iced your skin. Like an omen. But the day was sunny and golden with not an omen in sight, and 'if only' were the two most useless words in the language—Sienna knew that more than anyone.

And even if she had known—what could she have done that would have made things different? Nothing. She was as powerless as a leaf torn from its branch by a cruel autumn wind.

Yet her mood was light as she slipped into the back entrance of the Brooke Hotel, via the garden. The ivy-covered walkway was her favourite way into the building, for when you stood in the secret courtyard it was difficult to believe that you were right in the centre of London—with the hubbub and bustle of the busy streets only a stone's throw away.

Here the sounds of the city were muted and soft-ened by the tall, waving branches of trees which acted as a haven for all kinds of birds. Bees buzzed drows-ily around the flowers and little ladybirds landed on your bare flesh and sometimes nipped it if you weren't looking. These days she was essentially a city girl, but this place reminded her of a country child-hood which seemed another world away.

Sienna loved the Brooke. It was where she had fled to. Where she had been promoted. Where she had made the slightly scary decision to go freelance—but the hotel still provided the bulk of her work. As an events organiser, she organised weddings, birthday parties, book launches and bar mitzvahs—and her name was becoming well-known on the busy London social circuit. From fairly humble and untrained be-ginnings, she had certainly landed on her feet.

And if she ever stopped to think how she'd got here… Well, that was the whole point—she didn't ever think about it. Thinking never got you anywhere. It took you to all kinds of dark and disturbing places and in the end it changed precisely nothing. In life you just had to learn from your mistakes. To get through the bad times in the hope that there would be some good ones waiting round the corner. And there were. Of course there were.

Today, the dark onyx reception desk was massed with startling orange Bird of Paradise flowers mixed in with black irises and red lilies. It was a dramatic look, and not one favoured by shrinking violets—but then those kind of people didn't tend to stay here.

Money and power and a hungry desire for some-thing 'different' were the driving forces behind the screamingly influential clientele of the Brooke. Film-stars. Entrepreneurs. Royalty. Anyone who was anyone.

They all flocked to the converted eighteenth-century mansion where there was never an empty room. Where, as a client, you paid through the nose for luxury and discretion.

Sienna rode up in the penthouse elevator. She was meeting a Mr Altair, and before she met a client she always allowed herself a little daydream about just what kind of party they would want. A themed affair, perhaps? Like the time she had decked out a marquee to recreate a French circus—and had only just managed to persuade the trapeze artist not to flounce off in a huff because he hadn't had star billing!

Or the time she had crammed a ballroom with a thousand red roses for one of the most over-the-top engagement parties she had ever had a hand in.

Sienna smiled. Her job required that she had the organisational skills of an army general—combined with the smooth tongue of a career diplomat.

As the lift doors slid open, the door to the penthouse was opened by a tall, olive-skinned man. Some sixth sense should have told her then—but why would it? With his black eyes and the expensive suit which didn't *quite* disguise the gun in his breast pocket the man looked like any other foreign 'minder'. Which she supposed was the modern word for bodyguard—and she came across plenty of those in this line of work.

'Hello.' She smiled. 'My name is Sienna Baker and I have an appointment with Mr Altair.'

A flicker of something she couldn't quite put her

finger on passed over his impassive features, but he merely nodded and pushed the door to the apartment open. He stood by to let her pass but did not follow her inside, and as the door clicked shut behind her Sienna felt inexplicably apprehensive. As if she was closed in. Trapped. Though agoraphobia would be the last thing she should be suffering from in a room of these dimensions.

She looked around her, her senses swamped by the sudden crowding of different sensations which began to jostle for supremacy in her mind.

For a moment she was dazzled by the sheer impact of the light which spilled in from the enormous windows, and she screwed her eyes up in confusion as the faintest trace of a disturbingly familiar scent began to drift towards her. The exotic smell both tantalised her and began to make her stomach twist painfully, and she couldn't work out why.

And then she saw the man standing completely still with his back to her, silhouetted against the London skyline—tall and dark and lean and proud, as if he had been carved from some black and unforgiving rock—and Sienna felt the blood drain from her face as he moved, like a statue coming to life.

She sucked in a breath of disbelief as her eyes flickered over him, her mind screaming out its protest as she began to register every detail about him. The slick black hair with the faint wave to it. The broad shoulders and the long legs. The arrogant and autocratic stance. Oh, please, no. Please. No. But now the scent which pervaded the suite became more understandable—and wasn't smell supposed to be the most evocative of all the senses?

Did she whimper or make a sound? Was that why he had begun to turn around? And now the breath caught in her throat as she began to issue a silent and heartfelt prayer. She prayed like she hadn't done for a long, long time, since she had been begging some mysterious presence to take the pain away. If no one had been listening then, then let them be listening now.

Don't let it be him. Oh, please don't let it be him. But her heart plummeted like a stone as he turned to face her.

Hashim surveyed her with cold and glittering black eyes, acknowledging the heavy stab of desire in his loins with a grim kind of pleasure, remembering the splayed abandon of her legs the last time he had seen her, and the aching only increased.

He had long denied himself this moment because he had told himself that he could, but in the end desire had proved irresistible. Hashim despised the weakness which made him want her, yet he embraced it, too. And he intended to savour every moment of it. This woman who had deceived him would pay, and she would pay with her body!

He let the narrowed ebony gleam of his eyes linger on her figure, to see if time had marred its perfection, but it was as firm and as lushly slim as a prized young

Saluki—the silky-sleek hunting dogs much favoured by the tribes of his native land.

It was hard to pin down what made her quite so desirable—for hers was not a fashionable look. She was too petite and curvy for modern tastes, yet her body was to die for. And if you added to that the ingredients of innocence and sensuality…

Innocence!

Hashim's mouth hardened as he thought of what a sham appearances could be.

He let his gaze drift upwards, to her face. How white her skin was, he observed with impartial inter-est—and how contrasting the deep rose of her lips. Ah, those lips! One of the very first things he had noticed about her had been her natural pout, which some women spent thousands of dollars at plastic sur-geons trying to recreate.

Now those same lips trembled under his scrutiny, and he longed to crush their petal softness beneath the hard, seeking warmth of his own. But that would have to wait…and the waiting would only increase his eventual pleasure.

'Sienna,' he murmured as the warm throb of blood beat between his legs.

The way he said it took her back to somewhere which was out of bounds, and her heart buckled with pain as she stared at the man she had once believed herself to be in love with.

He was both ugly and beautiful, his face unique—defined by hard contours and the ravages of warfare.

An exotic, foreign face. The cruel beak of a nose and harsh slash of his mouth only added to his allure, and those clever black eyes could make a woman feel as if he was slowly stripping her bare…

Seeing him again was a moment she had lived out in her mind over and over again—though not much lately, it was true. But wasn't it simply human nature to wonder how she would react if ever she saw him again? As time had passed she had convinced herself that the sobbing wreck of her early days had been replaced by a confident woman who would give him a cool smile and say, *Hashim! Well, long time no see!*

How wrong she had been. How very wrong and how very *stupid*. As if any woman could look at a man like that without wanting to melt into a helpless puddle of longing at his feet. But the longing was eclipsed by another emotion, and that was wariness…or was it *fear*? What the hell was he doing here?

'Hashim,' she whispered, like someone waking from a long dream. 'Is it really you?'

'It really is.' His hard eyes mocked her, enjoying her discomfiture in a way he had not enjoyed anything for a long time. 'You seem surprised, Sienna.'

'Surprise implies something pleasant,' she said shakily.

He arched heavy black brows in sardonic query. 'And this is not?'

'Of course it's not!' Nervously, she flicked her tongue over her lips to moisten them, and then wished she hadn't, for his black eyes were drawn to the movement as a snake to the charmer's pipe. 'I'm shocked—like anyone would be.'

'I disagree—a lot of women might be delighted to see a man who had once featured in their lives, but I guess it's different in your case.'

Her eyes pleaded with him to stop, but he did not, and his hard mouth twisted into a cruel imitation of a smile.

'I expect your past is always coming back to un-settle you in all kinds of ways—but you have only yourself to blame, my dear. If you didn't keep so many unsavoury secrets, then you might be able to sleep a little easier.' He allowed his eyes to linger on the exquisite swell of her breasts and the swift shaft of desire became blunted with the memory of be-trayal. His mouth hardened. 'Though I can't imagine any man letting *you* sleep easy at night.' Except maybe him. The mad, duped fool who had protected her and respected her. Who had cherished her as if she had been a delicate and priceless piece of por-celain.

And then seen her crushed into smithereens before his eyes.

But he was a fool no more...that day had gone...never to return.

Sienna wanted to tell him not to stare at her that way, but she knew if she did that then he would do it all the more. He was not a man to be thwarted or dictated to, and in his hard black eyes was the glitter of danger. She swallowed, terrified to ask the question because of what the answer might be. Until she told herself that this was just some horrible, unfortunate coincidence—it had to be...

Or was it? Suddenly she wasn't so sure. Did anything ever happen completely by chance?

'What are you doing here, Hashim?'

He thought how easily his name came to her lips. How little she realised the honour accorded to her by being able to speak it so freely where most women would dip their eyes in deference! Even the sophisticated women in his life—and there had been many—had always been slightly in awe of his power and position. He stared at her, and the anticipation of what he was about to do made his blood sing with pleasure. 'You know very well why I am here,' he reprimanded silkily.

For a second her world was suspended in a moment of disbelief as she was frozen by the stark sensual intent in his eyes. And it was as if just that one sizzling look had begun something which her unresisting body was powerless to stop. She shook her head, trying to stop the stealthy and hated shiver of desire. 'No, I don't.'

'Shame on you, Sienna—is this how you always react when you are booked in to have a business meeting? You are being paid to organise a party for me—remember?'

His soft, mocking words made her throat close over with fear and she swallowed it down. There was no way she could have any kind of meeting with him—business or otherwise. He must know that!

'No!' she said, as calmly as she could. But as she shook her head the heavy weight of her piled-up hair wobbled, as if itching to cascade down her back. 'That's not what I meant, and you know it!' She looked around her with slight desperation, as if any minute now she would suddenly wake up and discover that the whole incident had been some ghastly nightmare. 'I'm supposed to be meeting a Mr Altair! Not you.'

He gave a cold smile. 'But "Mr Altair" *is* me, Sienna. Didn't you realise?' His smile grew even colder, even though the undulating movement of her hair made him ache to unpin it and set it free. Free to tumble onto the warm nakedness of his chest. And his belly…

'Altair is one of my many aliases,' he drawled. 'Surely I used it when I knew you?'

'No,' she whispered. 'No, you didn't.'

'Ah. So much changes with the passage of time, does it not, Sienna? What else has changed, I wonder?'

She felt like a woman who had woken up in an alien place, where all the rules of survival had changed, and she knew that she had to take control—not just of herself but of the situation, too. She was no longer a young girl, besotted and completely fixated by a man who was light-years away from her in terms of experience. The wrong man, she reminded herself painfully.

With an effort, she gave him a smile. A rueful, grown-up smile. 'Look, Hashim, I presume that now you've seen me you've changed your mind. We aren't going to be able to do this—you know we aren't.'

His eyes glittered with provocation. 'To what… precisely…do you refer? What aren't we going to be able to *do*, Sienna?'

She didn't rise to the sexual taunt. If she kept it on a business level then she might be safe—but if she allowed the discussion to stray into the personal or—even worse—the past, then she really was in danger.

'But what are you doing here?' she questioned, still with the last vague hope that things were not what they seemed. 'When you always stay at the Granchester?'

'Maybe I find that the memories there are too tainted,' he mocked. 'Or maybe I find that I just can't resist the attractions on offer here…' Once again he let his eyes linger with insolent hunger on the swell of her magnificent breasts. 'Your…reputation in the capital is growing, Sienna,' he added silkily.

She didn't suppose he was alluding to her backlog of satisfied clients. It was not a compliment at all, but a thinly veiled insult, implying…implying… Oh, she knew damn well what he was implying! Feeling as though her lungs had been scorched, she sucked in a breath to steady herself. 'But presumably you're not expecting me to work with you,' she said quietly.

He gave a heady, husky laugh of anticipation. 'For an employee you sure as hell make a lot of presumptions. It could get you into a lot of trouble if you're not careful.'

She had forgotten what a curious mixture he was, of the ancient and the modern, the forward-thinking and the ludicrously old-fashioned. He was one of the most intelligent men she had ever met—so why the hell was he deliberately misunderstanding her reservations? 'Oh, Hashim—don't be so…dense!'

'Dense?' He tilted his chin imperiously and his eyes narrowed into glittering ebony shards. 'You dare to address *me*—a *sheikh*—in such a way?'

In the past he had never pulled rank—but then he hadn't needed to. She hadn't cared about his position—hadn't even known about it to start with. And by the time she did it hadn't mattered. Or at least she'd thought it hadn't—but that was yet another indication of just how out of her depth she had been. Because of course it had.

It had mattered a lot.

CHAPTER TWO

SHE should never have met him, of course, for theirs were two such different paths in life—destined never to cross. But country girls sometimes went to live in big cities and became receptionists in super-smart hotels—the kind of places where you bumped into real-live sheikhs when you were on your way to work. Just like a fairy tale. And sometimes the fairy tale came true—but what it was easy to forget was that there was always a dark side to the story.

Sienna had gone to London for the usual reasons—and then some more. In the midst of crisis she had needed money and a solution. And after that... Well, after that she had needed to forget. And, as well as offering her anonymity, the big city had also offered her the opportunity to work her way up the ladder in the hotel industry—and to live rent-free in one of the most expensive parts of London. A perk which had made up for the long and unsociable hours.

The first time she had seen Hashim, Sienna had been on her way to the hotel for a late shift. It had been a beautiful day, and she'd been enjoying the sunshine.

She'd been wearing nothing out of the ordinary—a floaty kind of summer dress—but her hair had been

17

down and she'd walked with the unconscious vigour of youth. In her daydream she'd barely noticed the slight commotion of people milling around the dark-windowed limousine of the world-renowned Granchester Hotel.

And then she had seen the figure emerging from the car. He'd been tall, with a natural autocratic poise, dressed in a coolly pale suit which had made the dark olive of his skin look so silken. It had gleamed soft gold and contrasted with the hard ebony glitter of his eyes.

For a split-second as they'd looked at one another it had been like something out of one of the old-fashioned films she'd always been a sucker for. As if she had been waiting all her life to see just that man looking at her in just that intent and interested way. His eyes had narrowed as a bodyguard had shot an arm out in front of her, bringing her to a halt.

'What do you think you're doing?' she had protested, and the man had smiled a hard kind of smile, and then said something in a husky tongue which was foreign to her.

'Let her pass,' he clipped out, as if he was translating the command for her benefit, and the bodyguard grunted and moved aside. Sienna inclined her head.

'Thank you.' She walked off down the road, somehow aware that the black eyes watched her, burning into her back, branding her with their strange exotic power.

And then, a few weeks later, he came into the hotel and Sienna just froze.

He looked…she swallowed…he looked so vibrant…so *different*—as if someone had plucked a bright and very exotic bloom and placed it in a vase of white flowers. She could see people in the foyer giving him sly little glances, and others—women— giving not so shy ones. And his two bodyguards— ever-present in the background, solid as a brick wall and silently sending out messages to *keep away*.

Experience had made Sienna wary of men, and so her unexpected reaction to this one took her by surprise. When desire had never really touched you it was a bit earth-shattering when it did. 'Um, um…' She could feel her cheeks growing pink. How unprofessional! 'I mean, good morning, sir.'

Hashim's eyes narrowed with interest. It was the girl with the green eyes and the body! And what a body!

Carelessly, he flicked his hand to indicate that the bodyguards should remain where they were, and he moved forward to the desk himself, fully aware of the impact he was making as he stared down into her face. 'Hello again,' he said softly.

His accent was silky, rich and deep, and the tiny blush which had begun deepened to heat her cheeks. Her heart thumping in her chest as if it had just discovered how to beat, Sienna jabbed her finger at the booking diary. 'Can I…can I help you, sir?'

The side of him which had been indulged from the

cradle wanted to lower his head and whisper that, yes, she could spend the afternoon in bed with him—but her innocent blush meant that he had unconsciously moved her into a category of women with whom it was not acceptable to flirt outrageously.

'I am meeting one of your guests here for lunch,' he said instead.

'And the guest's name, sir?' she questioned, looking down at her booking list and wishing she could stop blushing.

He gave it, and saw her eyes widen—for the politician he was meeting was well known, and Hashim knew very well the potency of power and connections. He had lived with them all his life.

'He's waiting at the table, sir. I'll take you in to join him.'

She stood up to show him the way, and he enjoyed following her into the restaurant, so that he could watch her unobserved.

She was not tall, but he liked that—for he believed that a woman should look up to a man—and although her hips were narrow, her bottom was as curved as her breasts, and designed to be cupped by the warmth of a man's hand.

But it was her green eyes, shaped like almonds, and the pinkness of her cheeks and the rose pout of her lips which stayed in his mind. During lunch he gestured for one of his guards to approach, lowering his head to give an instruction in his native tongue, and the guard was dispatched to the reception desk to acquire her phone number.

But Sienna refused to give it. What a cheek—sending his henchman! And in a way it just confirmed her rather jaundiced view of men. She wished she could go on her break right then, but it wasn't for ages, and when he came out of the restaurant she was still sitting there.

She looked straight through him, as if he wasn't there—something which had never happened to him before. But he was too intrigued to be outraged, and some alien emotion directed his steps towards her.

'You wouldn't give me your phone number,' he mused.

'You didn't ask me.'

'And was that such an unforgivable sin?' he teased.

She turned her head away, unsure how to cope with him, this powerfully built and exotic man who was making her feel things she wasn't used to feeling.

'What is your name?' he asked, without warning, and she turned back to find herself imprisoned in the blazing ebony spotlight of his eyes.

'Sienna,' she whispered, as if he had sucked the word clean out of her, without her permission.

'Sienna,' he repeated softly, and nodded. 'So, are you going to have dinner with me, Sienna?'

Somewhere in the recess of her mind was the thought that staff *definitely* weren't supposed to fraternise with the guests—until she remembered that he wasn't actually a guest. And even further back was another thought—that she was rather good at getting out of her depth. 'I'm not sure.'

'Why not?' he questioned softly.

'Because I don't even know your name.'

'Ah! Did not one of your finest poets once ask: "What's in a name?"' His black eyes narrowed. 'My name is Sheikh Hashim Al Aswad.'

Sheikh? *Sheikh?* Something in his eyes made her stare at him, aghast. 'You're not really a sheikh, are you?'

'I'm afraid I am,' he replied gravely.

Sienna stared up at him. Now his dark looks and foreign air and the unmistakable aura of authority made sense. 'But what on earth would I wear?'

And he laughed. 'It doesn't matter,' he said truthfully. 'You are so young and so beautiful that you would look wonderful in anything.' Or nothing, of course.

That night he took her to a restaurant which overlooked the silver snake of the river which wound its way through the city. The stars outside seemed close enough to touch. And the evening felt magical enough for Sienna to feel that she could.

She had thought she might feel awkward and out of her depth, but instead she was so—*excited*, and determined to enjoy every second of it. Even the simple little cotton dress she chose seemed okay, because her thick dark hair reached almost to her waist, and she wore it loose and saw the narrow-eyed look of approval he gave and knew she'd got it just right.

It felt like an old-fashioned date was supposed to feel. Hashim ignored the fact that there were two armed bodyguards seated a few tables away, and more outside. This felt different, and he wasn't quite sure why. Because she seemed so transparently innocent?

'So tell me about yourself,' he instructed.

Sienna hesitated, wondering where to begin. Was this true lives or true confessions? She had once done something she didn't feel too great about—but that one-off act didn't define her as a person, surely? She'd probably never see him again after tonight—so why let him in on a secret which might ruin the evening?

She thought about what a man born to a sheikhdom would most like to hear. Well, she couldn't compete on a material front, that was for sure! She leaned forward and clasped her hands on the starched linen tablecloth, and tried to paint a picture of a very different life.

'I grew up in a little village. You know—a proper English village, with lambs gambolling around the meadows in the springtime and cherry blossom on the trees.'

'And in summer?'

'It rained!' She wriggled her shoulders. 'Well, actually, it didn't—it just seems to now, whenever I go back. But maybe that's because I'm an adult now. When I was little the sun always seemed to be shining and golden.' She stared into his face, thinking that she had never seen eyes quite so black. 'I suppose that most people's childhoods are like that. We view them through rose-tinted glasses.'

He thought not. Certainly his own had been nothing like that, but he would not describe it, nor compare the two. He would not have dreamed of expressing his own thoughts about growing up. Privacy was second nature to him and always had been—drilled into him from the very beginning. Instead, he picked up on the wisftfulness in her voice. 'If it was so idyllic, then why did you leave?'

Sienna fiddled with her napkin. 'Birds need to fly the nest.'

'Indeed they do.' His eyes narrowed. 'And is life outside the nest all you dreamed it would be?'

Sienna hesitated. It could be scary. It gave you opportunities, and they could be scarier still. 'Well, you gain freedom, of course—but you lose stability. I guess that's what life is like, though—gains and losses—hopefully it all balances out in the end.'

'You have a very wise head on such young shoulders,' he said gravely.

'You're making fun of me.'

'No.' He shook his head and gave a gentle smile. 'No, I am not. I find your attitude quite charming, if you must know. How old *are* you, by the way?'

Would he think her too young? *Too young for what, Sienna?* 'Nearly twenty.'

But he smiled. 'Only nearly?' he teased.

'Now you,' she said. 'What on earth do sheikhs *do*?'

His mouth twitched. She really *was* irresistible. 'Sometimes I ask myself the very same question. Mainly, they rule a country, and that involves much fighting and the quest for power—but they also oversee oil exports, which is why I am here.' *And they are surrounded by a wealth that most people couldn't begin to comprehend.* Especially not her.

Sienna crumbled a piece of unwanted bread. 'So where's home?'

For a moment he said nothing, and then gave an odd kind of smile. 'Qudamah is my home—but I come from a race of nomadic people.' His black eyes glittered. 'We do not settle easily.'

If she had been older she would have recognised that he was defining boundaries—but as it was his romantic words simply fired up her already overworking imagination.

Later, in the darkened limousine, his hard thigh brushed against hers and Sienna could hardly breathe. But there was no kiss, merely the request—no, the *demand* that he see her again.

It all happened so fast—Hashim's life slipped into a different timescale and he found himself experiencing something which was unknown to him: a tumult of feelings which he was too seasoned and too cynical to call love. Yet his ancestors had been poets and sages, as well as warriors, and he was prepared to acknowledge that somehow Sienna touched a part of him which had before gone neglected. It was as if her innocence and her beauty had begun a slow melt of something he had not known was frozen.

Maybe it was his heart.

She trembled when he kissed her, and he could feel the tension of both eagerness and fear when he took her in his arms. It seemed unbelievable—given her age and her liberal Western upbringing—but something told him that his instinct was correct.

One evening his eyes burned into her as he stared down into her flushed face. 'You are innocent of men?' he demanded.

'Yes,' she admitted in a low voice, wondering if that admission would drive him away from her. 'Yes, I am.'

'Innocent virgin,' he moaned as he kissed her. '*My* innocent virgin.'

Of course that changed everything. The knowledge of her purity filled him with delight, but there was also the certainty that he now bore a heavy responsibility towards her. For a man whose life had been burdened with responsibility, it was another he could have done without—and yet he found himself embracing it.

He saw her whenever he could, wondering if the frequency of their meetings would remove some of the magic, but the magic remained. He had spent his life avoiding any kind of commitment, yet now he saw that as a deficiency, not a blessing.

He took her to discreet restaurants and she showed

him the hidden, secret places of the city. She made him feel alive. Never before had sex been denied him, but this was a self-imposed restraint, and he discovered that doing without something you really wanted could be unbearably erotic.

And yet her innocence made her suitable. Eminently suitable. Of course many bridges must first be crossed, and the first of those would be to introduce her to his family. But without pressure on either side. On neutral territory.

'How would you like to accompany me to a wedding, sweet Sienna?' he asked her one afternoon, looping his arms around her waist.

Sienna looked up into his black eyes. 'Whose? Where? When?'

'My cousin's,' he murmured. 'In the South of France, next month. My mother and sisters will be there.' He glittered a smile at her. 'Will you come as my guest?'

Sienna knew that this was important. A statement. An indication that things were getting serious. She gave him a slow smile of delight. 'I'd love to,' she said simply.

Hashim spoke to one of his aides. 'Will you arrange it, please?'

'But, Your Highness, you are quite sure?'

Hashim frowned. He would not be dictated to! The history of his country was studded with examples of sheikhs who had taken commoners as wives...

But a couple of days later there was a rap on the

door when he was working in his study, and Hashim looked up to see the Arctic dark eyes of his equerry, who was carrying what looked like a glossy magazine between his fingers, as if it was contaminated.

'Yes, what is it, Abdul-Aziz?' he demanded imperiously. 'I am going out shortly.'

His equerry's face was grim. 'Before you do, Your Highness, there is something I must draw your attention to.'

For the umpteenth time, Sienna raked her hands back through her hair—fizzing over with a mixture of excitement and nerves.

Hashim was sending a car for her and they were having dinner at the Granchester Hotel, where he was staying.

She was still reeling from his invitation to the family wedding—so excited at the prospect of going public with him that she hadn't had time to worry about what she was going to say to his mother.

She would just be herself, without artifice or airs, for that was who Hashim liked her to be. She gave herself a little shiver of excitement as she walked up the imposing marble stairs of the Granchester Hotel.

But Hashim was not there to greet her, and neither were any of his staff. Not even the hatchet-faced Abdul-Aziz. Instead, she got a message delivered with a rather knowing look from the receptionist as she was directed up to his suite.

It isn't the way you think it is! Sienna wanted to

say to her. *Hashim has never treated me with anything but respect!* But as she rode up in the private lift which led to the penthouse she wondered why he had changed the pattern of their meetings.

Hashim opened the door himself, and Sienna was taken aback when she saw him—for she had never seen him dressed like this before. Tonight he looked exactly as she had imagined a sheikh *would* look.

Gone were the immaculate hand-made suits he usually favoured—which contrasted with his exotic looks and made him such a tantalising combination of East and West. Instead he was wearing a pair of filmy silk trousers in a deep claret colour, with a silky top in the same material. The rich hue made the most of his exotic colouring, and Sienna felt the roof of her mouth dry—for he was barefoot and the shirt was open, and through it she could see his olive hair-roughened chest, darkened with contours of muscle and sinew.

She had never been confronted quite so vividly by his overt masculinity before, and her heart gave a startled little leap as she found herself wondering if he was actually wearing any underwear at all.

But it was more than his state of undress which unsettled her—for his eyes looked *dangerous* tonight. Steely and brittle. Like jet. Something stopped her from hurling herself into his arms in the breathless way which always made him laugh—and she wasn't sure whether it was excitement or fear. But why on earth would she be frightened?

'You look beautiful tonight, Sienna,' he said deliberately.

Were nerves getting the better of her, or was there an odd undertone to his voice? 'Thank you. I—' But her words were lost beneath the hard, heady pressure of his mouth, for he had pulled her into his arms without warning and had begun to kiss her in a way which took her breath away. 'Hashim!' she gasped.

Her mouth opened up beneath his and it was enough to ignite all the fire and the fury which had been smouldering away inside him. He kissed her until she was melting and aching and moaning beneath his seasoned touch, and only then did he lift his head and glitter a hard, bright question down at her.

'Hashim…what?' he questioned huskily, moving his mouth to her throat to trace a featherlight kiss along its silken path.

It would be madness to protest that he had never kissed her like this before—not when she had spent hours wondering why.

'Oh-oh-oh!' She shuddered as he lightly drifted his hand over her breast.

A grim, silent smile of triumph curved his hard lips as his fingertips returned to whisper over their pert lushness. 'Oh, what, Sienna?' came the silken query. 'Is that good?'

'Oh! *Oh!*' she gasped. 'So good!'

A tiny pulse flickered in the centre of one tensed olive cheek. 'Tell me what it is you want,' he grated.

Instinct took over from reservation and sent the

words spilling out of their own accord. 'That,' she sighed, as his fingers brushed fleetingly against the aching mounds of her breasts. 'That's what I want!'

He cupped the magnificent swell in his hand and rubbed a slow and deliberate circle with his thumb. 'Like *this*, you mean?'

She nodded as pleasure constricted her throat into a tight, dry band.

'I can't hear you, Sienna,' he urged softly.

'Yes,' she moaned. 'Yes! Just like that. Oh, Hashim…'

How he had misjudged her! Oh, yes! He could feel her responsive body pressing close to his, and knew that if he put his hand up her skirt she would not stop him. How far would she let him go in public? Would she let him unzip himself and plunge right in? Probably.

'You want that I should make love to you by the lift?' he demanded hotly.

In some dim recess of her mind she was aware that he sounded almost…*harsh*…*disapproving*… But maybe that was because he had been holding back for so long. Didn't they say that men had difficulty controlling their sexual hunger? Sienna drew back and swallowed breathlessly, lifting the palm of her hand to touch his rugged face, but it looked oddly cold and forbidding. Obviously he was holding himself tightly in check and she must not make him wait any longer—he had played the gentleman to her heart's content. It was time.

'Let's go to bed,' she whispered daringly.

His mouth hardened. 'Yes,' agreed Hashim, in an odd kind of voice. 'Why don't we?'

Without warning he shut the door with an echoing slam, then picked her up and carried her towards a vast double bed which was covered with a lavish embroidered gold coverlet.

'Fit for a king!' Sienna murmured with delight, but there was no answering smile in his eyes as he put her down on it.

'Only a sheikh this time, I'm afraid,' he responded tonelessly. 'Are you disappointed?'

She wanted to ask him if something was wrong, but by then he had come to lie down beside her and her last reservations melted away.

'Now, then,' he said decisively, and began to unbutton her dress, a pure feral smile of hunger emphasising the deep lines around his mouth. 'Ah...' He sucked in a slow breath of pleasure as her breasts were revealed to him, spilling lushly pale from the pink lace which confined them. 'So firm. So tight. So taut. Like two rich, ripe fruits. Beautiful. So very, very beautiful. You have the most beautiful breasts that I have ever seen, Sienna. What a lucky man I am.'

Something in his words unsettled her—but any slight anxiety she experienced was allayed with the expert motion of his fingertips, and Sienna closed her eyes.

'Yes,' he murmured approvingly. 'Lie back and enjoy it.'

Oh, but he was so thoughtful. Beneath that steely exterior he cared for her own pleasure first and foremost. She felt him unclip her bra and give a shuddering sigh. Her eyelashes fluttered open and she surprised a look of almost…*reluctance*…on his face. But then he lowered his head towards her and she could feel the approaching warmth of his breath.

'Hashim…' She swallowed. She wasn't sure that he'd heard her. 'Hashim,' she said again, almost desperately this time, for more than anything she wanted him to kiss her, to whisper sweet words to accompany these erotic gestures.

'Shh,' he instructed silkily, for he knew from experience that conversation could break the mood and concentration. He knew what he wanted and he was going to allow nothing—*nothing*—to stop him from achieving it.

Sienna squirmed on the cold coverlet and the expert movement of his hands made her need for reassurance vanish. Her breasts had never felt like this before. As if they had swollen to twice their normal size and were prickling with excitement—the blood coursing through them so that the slightest touch sent shafts of pure pleasure spiralling through her. She squealed as his tongue licked against the sensitised flesh.

'You are very responsive for one so…*innocent*,' he observed against her puckered nipple.

Another shaft of pleasure so acute that it bordered

on pain shot through her, and she was aware of an empty, echoing longing, just crying out to be filled. 'A-am I?'

'Yes, you are. And now you will be more responsive still….'

Sienna's breath caught in her throat, for his hand was moving downwards now, inching towards the heated clamour—the very heart of where she most wanted to be touched—and Sienna silently prayed that he wouldn't stop.

'I won't,' he said roughly, and she realised that she must have spoken the words out loud.

'Hashim,' she whispered, letting her lips rest against the soft furnace of his skin. 'Hashim, I love you.'

For a moment he stilled, then shook his head very slightly, silencing her with his expert caress. He touched her molten and responsive heat with such delicate skill until she gasped in disbelief—like someone frantically seeking something only not quite sure what. Restlessly, her head moved from side to side as she stumbled towards a place of promise so beautiful that she was certain it could not really exist.

But it did. Oh, it did. She found it and fell into it, sobbing out her fulfilment, scarcely aware of Hashim pulling away from her. But, as reason and sanity began to seep back in, she realised that he was getting off the bed and moving away.

Over to the other side of the room and as far away from her as possible!

She blinked as she struggled to catch her breath. 'Hashim?' she croaked in confusion. 'Is anything wrong?'

'Wrong?' He paused before answering her question, sucking in a deep breath as he sought—successfully—to bring his desire under control, to be replaced with the slow simmer of rage. 'I think that we're through with playing games, don't you?'

Sienna sat up on the bed, aware that her clothing was in disarray, feeling somehow cheapened as she stared into the forbidding mask of his face. A Hashim she'd never seen before, and one she barely recognised. 'Why are you behaving like this?' she questioned in bewilderment. 'Don't you...don't you want to make love to me? Properly?'

'You think I would deign to contaminate myself by *entering* you?' he questioned insultingly. 'You who have fooled me!'

'I don't have a clue what you're talking about!' But some self-protective instinct made her begin to button her dress with trembling fingers.

'The sweet little virgin!' he ground out furiously. 'Like hell you are! Sweet little virgins don't take their clothes off and pose for pornographic photos!'

And then it all became horribly, horribly clear. That calendar. Those twelve photos. Oh, those wretched, wretched photos.

Sienna flinched and let out a shuddering sigh. 'You've seen them?'

Had there perhaps been some insane part of him

which had been hoping that it was all a mistake—that she had a secret identical sister waiting in the wings, perhaps? Because, if so, that futile thought was banished by the look of guilt on her face.

His hopes and dreams for what might have been now crumbled before his eyes like desert dust as he realised his mistake. He had believed her to be the woman he *wanted* her to be, not the woman she really was. He had been sucked in by her beauty and her air of innocence. Oh, what a fool he had been!

'Yes, I've seen them!' he grated, remembering that he had been about to introduce her to his family! That he had actually been entertaining thoughts of her as a future bride. Fool!

'Hashim—please—it isn't how it looks,' she said desperately.

She had agreed to do the calendar as a one-off to get her mother the operation she'd needed. Her mother had been crippled with pain and facing ruin, and the badly needed operation had been expensive. It had been an unconventional way to get the money, yes—but the only way which had been open to her at the time. And surely if Hashim realised how *desperate* she had felt. How *hopeless* her mother's predicament…

'Please, Hashim…I can explain—'

'What? How you came to be rubbing your breasts and simulating *orgasm*?' he cut in brutally, but despite his disgust he nevertheless felt the hard leap of desire. For even though their existence destroyed any

future between them, he was not hypocritical enough
to deny that they were magnificent photographs. 'You
think that there is any acceptable explanation for
that?' he snapped.

'It isn't—'

But his rage was such that he barely heard her. 'On
the head of my camel you are a magnificent actress—
I commend you for that! You have succeeded in fool-
ing me. And you have lied to me,' he added bitterly,
remembering the way she had told him that she was
a virgin—and that she *loved* him.

'I did not lie to you! I just…' She looked at him
and shrugged her shoulders helplessly. 'Couldn't
think of the right time to tell you.'

'But there would never have been a right time! In
my culture, such conduct from the consort to the
Sheikh would be utterly repellent—surely you must
have known that?'

Sienna stared at him. Of course she had. Was that
another reason why she had buried it away? As if by
doing that she could pretend it had never happened?
So that she wouldn't have to face the repercussions
of her actions? Could carry on living in her little fantasy world with Hashim—untouched by the past and
untroubled by the future? But had she ever imagined
that the outcome would be any different from this?
That there would be some magical, fairy-tale solution
despite what she'd done?

No. Hashim would never forgive her.

The reality of seeing the contempt in his black eyes

was almost too much to bear, and Sienna stood up and picked up her shoes, her hair falling down over her face, concealing her pain from him.

But she paused by the door, lifting her gaze to his, unable to suppress the tiny flicker of hope which stubbornly refused to die.

'Is that it, then, Hashim? Is it…over?'

'Over?' His mouth hardened, for he wanted to wound her. To hurt her as she had hurt him. To destroy her dreams as she had destroyed his. 'I think you forget yourself. Did you ever expect that it would be anything other than a very temporary diversion?' he questioned imperiously. 'For I am the Sheikh and you are but a commoner.' His made his final thrust. 'A true commoner.'

CHAPTER THREE

How painful the past could be.

But as the mists of memory cleared, and Sienna looked into Hashim's steely black eyes, the pain came flooding back as if the years in between had never happened.

She remembered the way she had stumbled from his suite that evening, the tears beginning to slip from beneath her eyelids. Somehow she had made it home and howled into her pillow like a wounded animal. She had never known that it was possible to cry that much. Or to hurt that much. To be revolted by the thought of food and want only to sleep—but sleep had never seemed to come, and when it had, it mocked her with images of the dark face she had grown to love so much.

For the first and only time in her life she had understood the meaning of the word heartbreak—and she never wanted to experience it again.

It had taken her countless months to put her life back on track, to rejoin the human race. But a lot had changed since then—and most importantly *she* had changed. She was no longer the innocent young girl who didn't have a clue about life or how to handle men.

Just keep telling yourself that, she thought, with

more than a hint of desperation as she met his glittering stare.

'You're remembering the last time we saw each other,' he observed, an odd kind of note in his voice.

Had her face given her away? Maybe he had read in it her vulnerability and her anguish. 'How could I not?' she questioned, trying to keep her voice from shaking. 'I only have to look at you and it all comes flooding back.'

He stared at her and his black eyes were as hard as jet. Did she imagine that it was any different for him? He felt the hard leap of desire. 'So it does,' he agreed softly.

'Maybe we should try a joint counselling session,' she suggested, trying to keep it light. 'You know— like people who want to stop smoking.'

How flippant she sounded, he thought—and how cynical. Were those traits that she had kept cleverly hidden from him? And why not? Had she not been a woman adept in the art of concealment? 'But maybe I'm not ready to stop,' he said deliberately.

Sienna felt an odd kind of lump in her throat, and something both seductive and yet infinitely threatening hovered unseen and unspoken in the air. Now her voice did tremble. 'And wh—what's that supposed to mean?'

'Well, at least for you it was a…how shall I put this?' A cruel kind of smile lifted the corners of his lips. 'A satisfying encounter.'

His implication was very plain and very insulting, but it wasn't even true—or at least not in the way that

mattered. Maybe in one sense it had been satisfying—
on a purely physical level, yes—but on an emotional
one it had been as barren as one of the deserts in his
homeland. Fulfilment without tenderness was never
satisfying for a woman, and it had left her empty—
as if he'd ripped out an essential part of her and carried it off with him. 'Is that how you would describe
it?' she questioned bleakly.

'Wouldn't you?' he mocked.

'Not really, no.' She looked into the cold black
eyes and knew that he would never understand in a
million years—nor even want to try. Why would he?
Sienna shook her head, hoping to drive away some
of the sadness. 'Anyway, what's the point in discuss-
ing it? Things have moved on.'

His face remained impassive, but inside he felt the
flicker of anger mixed into a potent cocktail with sexual hunger and anticipation. She had fooled him once,
but never again! Did she really think for a moment
that now that he had her in his sights he was about
to let her go? Did she not realise what he wanted?
That he had come here to achieve just this?

But, like the expert hunter he was, he knew that
there were many ways to play with your quarry. Had
she too regretted the abrupt end to that meeting?
Perhaps for her as well as for him there had been
bitter regrets that their lovemaking had not been complete?

'Yes, things have moved on,' he agreed. 'But they
seem to have brought us back to the same place. I am

here and you are here—so just what do you think we
ought to do about it?'

He took a step closer to her. He was close enough
now for her to study him properly, so that she could
see how much he had changed—though none of the
fundamentals had. He was still the most breathtak-
ingly masculine man she had ever laid eyes on. As if
he had stepped from another age and another time.
His own particular scent drifted up her nostrils—a
vital, spicy scent that spoke of raw virility and
reached out to the most feminine side of her.

Briefly, Sienna closed her eyes in helpless recognition, and when she opened them again it was to see
the warm ebony fire in his. She could feel herself
drawn to him. Like a child who had been left outside
in the cold for too long. He promised the certainty of
warmth. Of comfort. And security.

She wasn't aware that he had moved again, but he
must have done—please God it hadn't been her—
because suddenly she was in his arms, her senses not
giving her time to question her sanity as he bent his
head to graze his lips across hers.

It was electric. Like fire. Ice. All extremes which
could shock the system to its very core—that was
Hashim's kiss. It awakened in her something which
had lain dormant, sleeping since the last time she had
been in his arms. Back then she had—in her naiv-
ety—imagined that all kisses would press the button
to instant sensual combustion, but in the interim she
had discovered how way off the mark she had been.

His expert lips were both hard and soft, seeking yet

commanding—and they tasted sweeter than the richest honey. Her own opened beneath them, to taste the warmth, to feel the seductive slide of his tongue into the moist interior of her mouth, and she gasped, buckled, so that his arms caught her against him, imprisoning her in an iron-hard grip which made her melt against him.

A great wave of longing swept through her. Physical—oh, yes—but something else besides. Something which was infinitely more powerful and far more dangerous. As if Hashim alone could fill some emotional space which seemed ever-constant inside her.

For countless seconds she felt the rush of blood and the clamour of response—the warm, primitive throb of blood as it centred and pooled at a place which made her ache. She felt one of his hands reach down to cup her buttock, and silently she begged him to move his fingers round, to delve into that secret place once more.

He seemed to read her thoughts—for he laughed as he moved his hand, teasingly drifting his fingers across her aching mound. She moaned in sweet response. He murmured something in a tongue which was foreign to her, but the mocking and triumphant tone of his words spilled over her heated senses like icy water and Sienna froze in disbelief.

What the hell was she doing?

With a wrenching effort she tore herself away, staring at him wide-eyed. Her breathing was ragged and her pulse was racing like a piston as she struggled to calm herself, smoothing down her dress frantically. Her face was on fire, and so, too—surely—was her heart. 'What the hell do you think you're doing?'

His smile was arrogant, though his eyes were cold. 'Exactly what you wanted me to do.'

'No!'

'Yes. You are hungry for me,' he taunted. 'I could do it to you right now and you would not stop me.'

Too angry and uncaring to think of the consequences, Sienna raised her hand as if to strike him, but he reacted instantly—quicker and more deadly than a cobra as he caught her wrist in his hand.

'You dare to strike the Sheikh?' he thundered.

'You dare to foist yourself on me?'

'Foist?' Giving a cruel laugh, he dropped her hand. He had demonstrated his superior speed and dexterity—she would not be fool enough to try that again. 'I can think of many different words to describe a woman grinding her hips against a man in silent plea to have him enter her—but foist is not one which springs to mind.'

She felt the flush of mortification. 'You…you…'

'Oh, spare me your empty insults, Sienna. They count for absolutely nothing when we both know that what I say is true. You want me,' he stated flatly.

'Don't flatter yourself!'

'Ah! Denial is such a powerful force, is it not?' he mused. 'Especially in women.'

As well as weaving subtle mazes with his clever words, was he telling the truth? Did she want him still? Maybe physically, yes. But emotionally—never!

'Just because you know which buttons to press, and all the ways to seduce a woman—'

'Now you are flattering *me*,' he interposed cruelly.

'It doesn't mean she necessarily *wants you*,' she stormed. 'It just means that her body is reacting as it has been conditioned to do by nature—there's a world of difference.'

'And do you turn on so easily for all men?'

'You're disgusting!'

'You have grown fiery,' he observed, noticing that she had chosen not to answer the question—though his arrogant pride would not allow him to believe that she would melt for another man in quite the way she did for him. 'Very fiery. Yes. I like that in a woman.'

'But I'm not looking for your approval. I have grown up, Hashim—I'm no longer the docile young girl who thought you were the greatest thing since sliced bread!'

It was both the right thing and the wrong thing to say, for while it burst the strangely seductive bubble of thwarted desire, it reminded him of her lying and cheating and duplicity.

'Yes, so docile,' he hissed like a rattlesnake. 'So young and so *innocent*! Like hell you were.'

She stared at the stark condemnation which was sparking from his eyes. He had judged her, and found her wanting. And, damn him, he was right—she *was* still wanting. Wanting him. 'Oh, Hashim, I was innocent in so many ways,' she said, her voice sad now. 'Why don't we forget the whole thing? Let me just walk out of this door right now and out of your life for ever.'

Was she mad? Did she not recognise his intent, nor realise that when he desired something it was always his for the taking? His mouth hardened. No, of course she hadn't recognised it—how could she when she had never seen it before? Her experience with him had been bizarre—and unique. Five years ago he had found himself bewitched by her and he had tempered his usual autocratic wishes—except that it had seemed to happen without any conscious effort on his part.

Now let her see the real Hashim! Who treated women as they liked to be treated! If you were cold and disdainful it seemed to make them want you more—never was a woman more giving in the bed-room than to a man who had treated her with contempt.

'I think you forget yourself,' he said icily. 'I have hired your services and therefore you will behave as such. You will show me respect and listen to my wishes.'

'Respect?' she echoed. 'Are you out of your mind?'

'Yes, respect,' he ground out. 'That is if you know the meaning of the word.'

Sienna blinked as a tremor of fear ran through her. Surely he didn't think…didn't think… She drew in a deep breath. Appeal to his sense of reason, she told herself. He is a powerful and successful man, and surely he will understand that it would be folly to extend this torturous interview for a second longer than necessary.

'Hashim,' she said quietly. 'You can't honestly expect me to organise a party for you.'

'Why not?'

'Because…because there's too much history between us!'

'Now you flatter *yourself*,' he bit back. 'A few shared outings does not qualify as history. Nor does the fact that you opened your legs for me.' He saw her face drain of all colour, but he pressed on ruthlessly. 'But it is your reputation that has excited my interest.' He paused deliberately. 'Your reputation is admirable, Sienna—at least in a purely professional sense. Your work is highly regarded and I want you to organise a party for me.'

'*Want* or demand?' she questioned.

'The interpretation is yours.'

'And if I refuse?' she questioned quietly.

'Don't go there,' he warned softly.

'I have nothing to lose by turning you down.' And everything to gain. Like her sanity.

'You don't think so? On what grounds? And could you cope with the consequences of your action?'

Sienna wrinkled her nose. 'Consequences?'

'Sure. I would inform the manager here of my extreme *displeasure* that you had reneged on an agreement. How would you explain it to him? Do tell, for it fascinates me.' The black eyes challenged her.

Appeal to him. Ask him nicely. And even though

the words threatened to choke her, she got them out.
'I'm hoping it won't come to that, Hashim.'

But he carried on as if she hadn't spoken. 'Would
you explain that I'd once felt you climax beneath my
fingers? I'm sure he'd be *very* interested to hear
that—it might even turn him on—but do you think it
qualifies you to refuse my request?'

'Don't be so disgusting!'

'That's twice you've used that word,' he mused.
'You think sexuality is disgusting? How you surprise
me—since your own must have earned you a great
deal.' Had she blown all the money? he wondered.
And why in hell hadn't she capitalised more? Used
that amazing body to make herself a small fortune?
Become rich by exploiting her fabulous breasts, instead of fixing up other people's parties?

Sienna tried one last time. 'You are right—my reputation *is* good *and* well-established. So much so that
I can afford to turn you down!'

'People will hear—for I will make sure of it. And
they will wonder and ask you why. What will you
say to them? Will you lie, Sienna? Stupid question—
of course you will!'

She shook her head. 'I could say that we dated a
couple of years ago—I could…pretend.' She stumbled on her ironic use of the word. 'Pretend that I
would find it too painful to work for you.'

'And you will look foolish.'

'I can live with that.'

'You may not have the luxury of making that decision.' A look of determination hardened his eyes to

jet. 'Either you work for me or your career is over. That much you can believe.'

There was a pause. 'This is *London*—in the twenty-first century,' she told him, her voice rising in disbelief. 'Not some desert kingdom where your word is law! You may be a rich and powerful man, but in the end you're just a client. Same as any other,' she finished defiantly.

Her spirit and resistance was making his hunger grow—did she not realise that either? 'You can stand there and attempt to argue with me all day, but it will make no difference in the end. For I mean what I say, Sienna—if you do not accept this commission, then I will ruin you.'

'*Ruin* me?' Her laugh was high, and slightly hysterical. 'Even if you could—' Something was beginning to tell her that his threat was not an idle one. 'Even if you could—why would you?'

'Because you are like a dark stain in my memory,' he breathed. 'An encounter I should never have had, but which I cannot close the book on until it has been brought to its rightful conclusion.'

The meaning of his words was beginning to sink in, but Sienna didn't quite believe it—didn't dare believe it. She could hear the deafening pound of her heartbeat. 'And what conclusion is that?'

There was a pause, and he captured her eyes in mocking taunt. 'You only have to say the word, Sienna, and we can have an action replay. We can put an end to the business we started five years ago.' Deliberately he stroked his palm down the muscular flank of his thigh and his eyes became narrowed, opaque. 'Like right now, if you like.'

His heartless words tore into her and Sienna recoiled from the blatant sexuality which shimmered from him like a halo. 'Are you suggesting...suggesting that I go to *bed* with you?'

'I'm not particularly fussy about the venue,' he drawled, and nodded his dark head in the direction of a sumptuous scarlet velvet *chaise-longue*. 'That might provide a stimulating setting, don't you think? Ever done it on one of those?'

The question made her feel cheap, but presumably that had been his intention. 'You have to be out of your mind,' she breathed.

'My mind has nothing to do with it,' he said silkily. 'So what do you say, Sienna—are going to risk all you've worked for going up in smoke, or are you going to do the sensible thing and accept the commission?'

Sensible? She suspected that jumping off a high cliff would have been more sensible, but Sienna cared desperately about the career she had worked so hard for. Her job relied almost entirely on word-of-mouth recommendations, and even if she fudged the real reasons for her reluctance to work for Hashim it would reflect badly on her. Very badly. People might start to think she had issues...that she was difficult to work with...

Did she have a choice?

No.

But if she was to be forced into a corner by his

autocratic will, then it was vital that she stopped behaving like a victim. Was she going to let him think
that she was scared of him? Cowed by him? Unable
to resist his sensual lure?

Never!

She nodded, drawing in a deep breath to give her
courage. 'Very well. Since you give me little choice
I will accept your commission. Satisfied?'

Hashim felt the stirring of excitement and anticipation. So he had won the first battle. A battle he had
not been expecting—but when he stopped to think
about it would instant capitulation have pleased him?
No. Nothing in life felt so good as something which
you had to fight for. 'Oh, no, Sienna—not at all satisfied. But I intend to be. Believe me when I tell you
that.'

She could hear the sultry note of desire which had
deepened his voice and decided to ignore it. Act pro-
fessionally, she reminded herself.

'Right,' she said coolly. 'Let's talk business—'

'Alas!'

He cut her short with an imperious wave of his
hand, though he didn't look or sound in the least bit
regretful.

'It cannot be now,' he murmured. 'For I have another appointment.'

Sienna stared at him, knowing that he could have
broken any darned appointment he wanted but was
choosing not to.

'So I will meet with you tomorrow to discuss the

details of my…*requirements*. Over dinner, of course,' he finished silkily.

She opened her mouth to say that she didn't do dinner with clients—except that would not have been true. Of course she did. She could not refuse him— he knew it and she knew it. Never in her life had she felt so helpless—like a fish with a great big hook in its mouth, just about to be reeled in by a heartless man who would like to gobble her up for breakfast.

'Very well. Dinner tomorrow it is. But you can wipe that triumphant smile off your face right now, Hashim—because the party is *all* you are getting and I mean that. There's no *way* I'm going to sleep with you!'

He said nothing, but gave a mocking smile, lifting a thick brown envelope from the ornate table beside the door and handing it to her. 'You may want to look at this,' he said.

Something in his eyes told her that this was nothing to do with the party, and her heart began to pound. She realised the contents at the exact moment she asked the question. 'What is it?'

'Oh, just an old calendar,' he drawled. 'You may recognise it.'

CHAPTER FOUR

SIENNA took the envelope downstairs to an empty office, then pulled out the calendar and stared at it dully. She hadn't seen it for a long, long time, and she was scarcely able to recognise herself in the sexy and provocative poses. She guessed that by today's standards it was pretty tame—but even so, nothing could disguise the earthy sensuality of the pictures.

They had flown her out to the Caribbean and dressed her in a variety of clothes—well, that wasn't strictly true, for the garments had all been designed to reveal rather than conceal, and they had all left her breasts on show. But that had been the whole point.

A filmy kaftan soaked with water. The bottom half of a low-slung bikini. A glittery thong. Sienna closed her eyes, but was unable to block out the vivid, Technicolor images.

She remembered her initial feeling of panic when they had told her what they wanted her to do. It had taken two rum punches before she had been able to lie face down in the sand and smoulder at the camera for the first of the shots.

And Sienna would never forget the moment she'd seen a Polaroid of her pouting glossy self, with sand-sprinkled skin and messy hair, and dark, peeking nipples. How she had given a little gasp of disbelief and been slightly repulsed by the glinting approval in the eyes of the art director.

Even now she could squirm at how naïve she had been. And even now the photos still had the power to shock her. With trembling fingers she shoved the calendar into her briefcase and let herself out of the hotel, taking in great gulps of hot and sticky summer air.

She spent a restless night, and the following day there was a constant dull ache at her temples. When she walked through the hotel foyer dressed for dinner she felt as if she was going to her own execution.

'Cheer up!' said the night porter. 'It might never happen! Going somewhere special, are you?'

Serena gave a wan smile. 'I'm having dinner with one of the guests in the Rainbow Room.'

'Lucky you!'

Sienna gave a hollow laugh. 'Yes, lucky me!' she echoed wryly. 'Still, at least it's beautifully air-conditioned up there. The temperature outside is claustrophobic.'

'Tell me about it!' said the porter.

Overnight a heatwave seemed to have descended on the capital, with all the force and stifling nature of a heavy fire blanket dropped down to envelop the city. The streets outside the cool hotel had been curiously airless, and Sienna's throat felt as tight as if she were still out in them.

As she rode up in the lift she stared at herself in the tinted mirror. The cool linen dress she wore still looked fresh, and the apricot hue of the glass gave her face a healthy-looking glow which completely belied the way she was feeling inside. But she was not going to let that overwhelm her. And she was not going to let him intimidate her.

The nude photos were part of her past. She couldn't change that, and neither could she rewrite her brief and confusing relationship with Hashim. But she had learned along the way, and that was the whole point of experience—good *or* bad.

Those had been pivotal events in her life which had made her into the cool and confident professional she was today. The change hadn't been easy, or instant, and she was not going to throw it all away because Hashim wanted to exact some kind of erotic payback for what had happened all those years ago. Or rather, what had *not* happened.

He despised her—he had made that perfectly clear—even though his body still wanted her. And on some level she still wanted him, too. But she would not allow herself to be picked up and used like some kind of convenience—to be tossed away at the earliest opportunity. And she would not repeat the mistakes of yesterday.

If he said things to rile or provoke her she would not rise to them. They could not have a scene if she didn't react to him. If he attempted to taunt her then she would just give him a cool and glacial smile. She would remain brisk, crisp and polite—in short, she would be utterly professional, and he would be unable to find fault with her.

Surprisingly, he was already at the table. She was a little early, and had expected him to be late, but, no, there he was. Waiting. Making the rest of the room shrink into insignificance. At a shadowed corner table sat two of the ever-present bodyguards.

Sienna walked towards him, looking for some kind of acknowledgement—a nod of his dark head in greeting—but there was nothing. Just those black eyes trained on her like twin barrels of a hunter's gun.

His hard, lean body was completely still, but his stance was tense, the powerful limbs coiled like a lion before pouncing. He seemed completely oblivious to the covert glances of the other diners in the room. To the almost tangible air of excitement among the normally celebrity-jaded waiters.

Hashim watched her approach, helpless and yet furious with himself for being unable to suppress the instant leap of lust he felt, for he had trained himself to control his desires. To be master of his wants and needs—not servant to them. A man who could control his sexual hunger was all-powerful, for sex made men weak. And his control had never failed him. How else could he have so ruthlessly given Sienna pleasure and then denied himself the relief of his own body? And bitterly regretted it ever since!

Yet on one level she remained a mystery to him. He had known women more beautiful than her—so what was the secret of her particular allure? The seductive sway of her hips? The too-big eyes which looked like those of a startled deer? Or just the fact that he had never had her when other men had? That he had paid homage to her virginity only to have its falseness revealed to him in the most humiliating way of all.

He let his eyes rove over the breasts themselves—so proud and magnificent and full. Yet she was hiding her most marketable asset beneath that rather unremarkable linen dress. His lips curled. How he hated linen—surely the most unflattering material a woman could wear, with its coarse feel and its tendency to crumple. And surely it was a little late in the day for such unwelcome modesty?

Yet the very *familiarity* of seeing her again was taking him into the unknown realms of fantasy. The past was a place he did not revisit. At least never before now. His restless and nomadic nature saw no point to it. For him there was not the comfort—nor the danger—of long-standing friendships. His destiny was to stand alone.

Then why are you breaking your own rules? taunted a small voice in his head.

He did not rise to greet her when she got to the table, and, interestingly, this small lack of courtesy wounded her. Could he not just have pretended—gone through the motions of normality?

'Hello, Hashim,' she said, as calmly as possible.

'Sienna.' Not a flicker of emotion crossed over the diamond-hard features. 'Please sit down.'

'Thank you.' She glanced up at the waiter, who pulled her chair out, and then there was nowhere else to look other than into the enigmatic black eyes. Their dark light swept over her, and she felt a moment of sheer physical weakness until she remembered her vow of earlier. Professionalism. 'So.' She flicked him a quick smile. 'Where shall we begin?'

'So quick to do business?' he murmured.

'One should always strive for professionalism,' she answered coolly.

'Ironically, that is what Abdul-Aziz always says.'

Sienna remembered the aide who had seemed to so dislike her. 'And is he here with you now?'

Hashim shook his head. Hot-headedly, he had blamed his aide for showing him the calendar, even though he had only been doing his job. But for a while the Sheikh had seen him as a bearer of bad tidings—and he was as superstitious as the next Qudamah man. So he had sent him home, and in a way the split had been necessary—for the older man had begun to see himself in a role which was not befitting a royal aide. He had begun to love the fatherless Hashim as a son. And Hashim had no need of extra love.

'Abdul-Aziz was posted back to Qudamah,' he said. 'He is married now, with a son of his own.'

'*Married?*'

'Yes.' And then, because this exchange seemed almost too *cosy*, too familiar, he allowed his eyes to drift over her face. 'Aren't you going to thank me for the calendar?' he questioned deliberately.

She had wondered when he would get around to mentioning it, and she had practised her response until she had it word-perfect. 'No, I'm not. And if you continue to talk about it then I will walk out of here right now.'

He gave a faint smile. 'Then I guess we'd better get the ordering out of the way.'

She glanced down at the menu, which was like a blur though she knew it backwards. 'I'd like the Dover Sole, please. Grilled, no sauce. With a side salad.'

'The choice of a woman on a diet,' he observed.

'Not at all. A woman who is careful about what she eats, that's all.'

'Careful?' His black eyes glittered. 'How very curious. Not a word I would have associated with you.'

She leaned forward. Big mistake—for now she was in full range of his subtle, spicy scent, and it crept over her like sensual fingers. She sat right back again. 'Why don't we clear something up before we go any further? You don't know me. Maybe you never did—but you certainly don't now. So you aren't qualified to make any judgments about me. Understand?'

The waiter reappeared as Hashim glittered her a look which said *Aren't I?* Sienna watched as he gave the order quickly, almost impatiently—like someone who had spent much of his life eating in expensive restaurants and was bored by them. She guessed he had.

And now take charge, she told herself. Behave like you would with any other new client. She reached into her handbag and pulled out a notebook. He eyed it with distaste.

'Is that really necessary?' he questioned acidly.

'I'm afraid so. You wouldn't be very happy if I forgot everything you told me, would you? And so far you haven't told me anything.'

'But you look like you're interviewing me—and we're in a restaurant!'

'Well, you chose it.'

'I know I did—but would you have agreed to dine in my suite if I had asked you?'

'Not a snowball's chance in hell.' She looked at him, daring him to defy her. 'Presumably you wanted me to be a captive audience?'

Hashim's eyes narrowed as he considered her quickfire responses. Smart. And sassy. No matter how good an actress she was, she couldn't play smart unless she really *was* smart. 'Captive?' he mused. 'Yes, perhaps I did.' He imagined her tied to his bed with black satin ribbons, wearing nothing but scarlet underwear and a pair of matching high heels, and he felt the heavy stab of an erection.

'So, is it going to be a big party?' Sienna asked, cutting into his erotic thoughts.

'Party?' With a distracted movement of his shoulders Hashim brought himself back to the subject in hand with an effort. 'No. Very small. A private dinner party for ten.'

'And the guest list?'

'One of my assistants will organise that side of it. I am afraid that most of my guests will refuse to deal with a stranger.'

Defensively, Sienna picked up her water glass. 'In that case I'm surprised I'll be any use at all.'

'But that is where you are wrong. You will be responsible for the event itself,' he said. 'I'd like you to organise the music—I thought perhaps a string quartet. And the lighting—I like lots of candles, by the way. And the wine and the food—of which there must be an interesting and imaginative vegetarian selection. The mood of the evening will be down to you, Sienna. Everything you need you must ask for, and it will be supplied.'

How effortless everything was when you were rich! You snapped your fingers and got what you wanted. Sienna allowed herself a small smile. Well, not quite *everything*. He couldn't have *her*.

'And what kind of ambience do you want?' she questioned. 'Is there any particular reason why you're giving this party?'

There was one brief moment of hesitation. 'As a thank-you,' he said smoothly, running the tip of one finger reflectively along the soft linen of his napkin. 'For some of the many people in England who have done me favours.'

Bizarrely, Sienna found herself wondering if that

included sexual favours—but since his dark, lean looks were attracting all kinds of predatory glances maybe it wasn't such a bizarre thought after all. 'Have you thought which of the hotel's function rooms you'd like? There are several.' She looked at him expectantly. 'Or do you just want to me to choose?'

He stared at her. 'But that is the whole point, Sienna,' he said softly. 'I don't want it held here—or indeed in any hotel. A hotel is too impersonal for the needs of this particular event. I want you to find me a house.'

Sienna looked up from her pad and met the dark steel of his eyes. 'What kind of house?'

'A fine country house—with gardens and a view— a very *English* house. It should have at least ten bedrooms, so that my guests can stay overnight should they so desire it. There should be a lake which will magnify the light of the moon and double the number of stars. Somewhere that symbolises everything which is beautiful about your country. Can you do that for me, Sienna?'

The poetry of his words momentarily threw her, as did that fleeting, dreamy look which had softened his hard face, and she swallowed. 'How long have I got?'

'A month.'

'A *month*? That isn't long. Certainly not to find the kind of house you're looking for.'

'Are you saying you can't do it?'

'Oh, I can do it,' she said. 'But you might have trouble getting your guests there if they've only got four weeks. Important people have busy diaries—especially the kind of people I imagine you'll be inviting.'

He gave a low laugh. 'Please do not concern yourself on that score. They will attend,' he said softly. 'If I so wish it.'

'By royal command?' she mocked, resting her wrist against her water glass and enjoying the sudden cool sensation. 'Tell me—just out of interest—have you spent your whole life getting exactly what you want?'

'Material things, yes. That is, I imagine, what you meant?'

'It wasn't, actually.'

'No?' He studied the dark shadows beneath her eyes. Was he responsible for those? Or had some lover shared her bed last night—making use of her body and denying her sleep? He found himself unprepared for the dark jealousy which twisted his gut, and his voice hardened. 'Money is the preoccupation of most women,' he said harshly. 'Surely not even you would deny that?'

How cynical he sounded. Sienna felt a wave of something like regret wash over her—for she had only helped to convince him that women would do all kinds of things for money. She wished the food would arrive, so that she could eat it and go. Yet wasn't there a tiny part of her which was revelling in the opportunity to be this close to him again? To feast her eyes on a man she had once loved to distraction—and told him so.

Briefly she closed her eyes as she remembered whispering it to him, on that last, terrible evening. And the way he had just ignored her trembling statement.

Try and obliterate the past, she told herself, but she stared down at the food on her plate without really seeing it.

'You aren't really hungry at all, are you, Sienna?' he said, his silken voice weaving its way into her troubled thoughts.

He breathed her name in a way she remembered him once breathing it in passion, putting the emphasis on the last syllable and holding it in his mouth as if it were a mouthful of fine wine.

'Not really, no.' He was looking at her in a way which was making whispers of longing tiptoe over her flesh—and she had to snap out of it.

She needed to protect herself against his enchantment, and she found herself wondering how other women coped. Surely she couldn't be the only woman he bewitched with his curiously old-fashioned air of mastery and chauvinism? And women weren't *supposed* to be bewitched by qualities such as those. They were supposed to look for tolerance and compassion—not simply the desire to be swept off their feet by a flashing-eyed Alpha man.

She laid her fork down and pushed her plate away. 'Well, since we've tied up the business side of things, and neither of us looks as if we're about to tuck into the food, then you'll forgive me if I take my leave—'

'No.' The word was emphatic. 'I will not. You aren't going anywhere because I haven't finished with you. Not yet.'

Did he mean to make her sound disposable? she wondered. Like something he could just crumple up and throw away? And suddenly it wasn't easy not to be intimidated, to take charge and be calm and un-flappable—all the things she had learnt to do in order to survive and succeed.

Maybe this was one conversation she couldn't get out of having, and maybe it was a waste of time to try. Like having a tooth pulled—wasn't that ravaging moment of pain worth it just for the blessed relief you felt afterwards?

'Well, fire away, Hashim,' she said, using her last bit of bravado. 'And get whatever it is you want to say off your chest.'

He traced a thoughtful forefinger along the edge of his lips. 'I simply cannot understand why you chose obscurity,' he said.

She stared at him. 'Excuse me?'

He gestured towards her, as if he was about to in-troduce her to someone at a party. 'Oh, there is no doubt that you have become successful—'

'Why, thank you,' she said drily.

'But only in a purely *relative* sense.' His gaze was very steady. 'It puzzles me that you have stayed working in hotels.'

'Lots of girls do.'

'But lots of girls do not look the way you do.'

'Hashim, *please*—'

'You could have earned a fortune by capitalising on your body, and yet you chose this. So tell me…' His question hung on the air and Sienna waited breathlessly. When it came out it was disguised with the silken cloak of civility, but the look of disgust which hardened the ebony eyes told its own story. 'Why did you never pursue your career in topless modelling?'

CHAPTER FIVE

WHY did you never pursue your career in topless modelling?

With Hashim's critical question ringing in her ears, Sienna felt like someone who had put a piece of expensive lingerie away in a drawer, only to pull it out and discover that it had become faded and moth-eaten. He made her feel cheap. Tawdry. Something she hadn't felt for a long, long time, and she glanced around them, as if the other diners might have overheard.

'You worry that people might be listening?' A cruel smile curved his lips. 'So you have not boasted of your days working in *glamour*?' The word dripped with contempt. 'You are concerned about what others think, perhaps? I cannot believe *that*, Sienna—for why reveal your body if you are afraid of people finding out about it? Why allow men to feast their eyes on your nakedness if you then act coy about it?'

'I'm surprised you bother asking me questions to which you obviously have all the answers,' she said quietly. 'Or rather, you have *decided* you know the answers. You think I am a certain kind of woman—so why don't we just leave it at that?'

'Because I am…curious.'

Yes, of course he was. He was fascinated in the same way that people couldn't help themselves looking at a roadside crash—they didn't want to be part of it, but something compelled them to watch. 'Why do you think I didn't pursue it, Hashim?'

He shrugged. 'Because I suspect you saw that in the end it would work against you. Would spoil your greatest ambition of all.'

'And what ambition would that be?' she asked faintly.

The tip of his forefinger rested thoughtfully against the dark shadow of his jaw. 'I think that you saw the seamy side of the industry, as girls who expose themselves often do. You anticipated that real dangers existed—and so you decided to work in the real world instead. An honest though a much harder living. But I suspect that you found it even harder than you imagined, and so you looked for an escape—an easier way—easier even than taking your clothes off.'

Sienna flinched. 'Go on,' she said, in a pinched kind of voice.

'You realised that you had an extraordinary gift which few are given. The gift of beauty.' His voice became cold as he recalled how he had fallen for the oldest trick in the book. 'Sirens had it, and lured sailors to their death. Men are driven mad by beauty. And you decided to use it as women have used their youth and their looks since the beginning of time. As a bargaining tool.'

Sienna swallowed, willing herself to float out from

her body—to hover suspended in the air above them, looking down at this horrible little scene to hear the words of vitriol which were spitting from his lips.

'With you, presumably?'

He shrugged. 'With me, yes—or with anyone else who happened to fit the bill at the time. I do not flatter myself that I would not have been moved aside if somebody even richer than I had stepped into the frame. You wanted a wealthy benefactor and for that you decided to play the Cinderella role. You chose a humble job as a receptionist, where your beauty stood out like…' He frowned, as if he was trying to remember something, the ebony brows knitting together, and then his face cleared. 'Ah, yes! Like a diamond in the rough,' he said softly. 'Hoping and praying and plotting that someone would sweep in and take you away from all that.

'And I must say that you were very good,' he continued, eyeing her thoughtfully. 'Even I was taken in by your deceit. You really did come over as an innocent and unspoilt girl. In a way, I suppose I should commend you for your acting ability!'

'Your English is quite perfect, Hashim,' she said unsteadily.

'I know it is,' he agreed arrogantly. 'I had an English tutor as a young child, and I am as fluent in your language as I am in my own. But why do you change the subject, Sienna?'

'Why do you think?' She felt as she imagined battered wives might feel. That after a while the punches no longer seemed to hurt. Insult someone enough and eventually the slurs would simply run off their skin like water. Let him rant and have his poisonous say, and then it would be over.

He narrowed his eyes at her. 'And still you do not contradict me?'

'What's the point? You are the worst kind of bigot—for you do not open your mind to the possibility that you might be wrong. You have made your mind up that something is so—and therefore it must be. I'm a topless model without any morals, and now it seems I'm an old-fashioned gold-digger to boot! Nothing will change the way you view me—so why should I even bother trying?'

'Because you have no defence against what I say!' he accused.

'We aren't in a court of law!'

'No, but that is where you might have ended up!' he declared hotly. 'In the end you *did* make the right choice—even though you have had to work hard for a living. But the women who continue along that path so often end up compromised. Next time—or the time after that—the photos that you agreed to do would not have been so tasteful. You would have got older, and as your youth faded you would have become more desperate. Soon you would have accepted less and less for more and more. And one day you might have ended up fully naked on some garage mechanic's wall in one of those explicit shots—'

'You *bastard*!' she hissed.

'But that is where you are wrong, Sienna. Your barb does not offend me because it is untrue—my birth was completely legitimate. Whereas what I say to you *is* true. The facts are indisputable.'

Sienna lifted a hand to the waiter who had begun to hover anxiously on the periphery of her vision. 'A glass of red wine, please.'

'Yes, madam.'

'You did not storm off,' he observed. 'As I suspected you might.'

Sienna shook her head. Her legs would not have carried her anywhere. She took the wine from the waiter and drank a large mouthful. Gradually its warmth and vitality began to seep through veins which felt as though they had been injected with ice.

'Why does it bother you so?' she questioned. 'Haven't you had girlfriends with questionable pasts before?'

'Of course I have. But they did not pretend to be something they weren't.'

There had been women who had made no secret of their hunger for his body and his money. And there had been actresses, too—of course there had—including one who had starred in a film which had broken the mould at the time. Some of the critics had called it soft porn. But none of that had mattered—they had just been cheap flings. What he'd seen had been what he'd got, and he had accepted that.

With Sienna it had been different—or at least he'd thought it had. They had been much more serious about each other. And when the sordid truth had been revealed to him he had felt outraged. It had made him question himself—he who had never had to question anything.

To a man impervious to self-doubt it had been a hard lesson to learn—that his judgement was not infallible—but ultimately it had made him stronger. And if there had still been one small fragment of his character which had believed in the fantasy of the perfect woman, then she had banished it for ever. He would never make that mistake again.

'What if…?' Sienna hesitated, feeling as if she was fighting for more than just her self-respect. She couldn't bear it when he looked at her that way— with such cold condemnation written in his eyes. 'What if you could understand my reasons for having done the photos?'

'Greed is never difficult to understand!'

'You have to understand that it wasn't like that— it really wasn't! I needed the money urgently.' She sucked in a breath and it felt like hot fire scorching down her throat. Would he believe her? 'To pay for an operation for my mother.'

There was a pause, and then he said, 'Bravo!' He gave a small silent handclap and then looked around, an expression of mock amazement on his face. 'But what has happened to the violins?' he taunted sarcastically. 'I can't hear them. Are there hordes of orphans at the door, too—waiting for you to put food in their mouths?'

'It's true, I tell you—it's true!' She wanted to stand up and rush round and drum her fists against his chest. To shout and to rail against him despite all that she'd vowed. But she couldn't—was that another reason why he had chosen the restaurant? To protect himself from an emotional scene? To enable him to insult her as much as he liked, knowing that she wouldn't be able to fight back?

'Whether you choose to believe me or not is up to you—but I'm not lying to you. Why don't you have one of your henchmen run a check on me?'

His eyes narrowed. 'What kind of operation? Cosmetic surgery, perhaps? Was she once as beautiful as you, Sienna, and could not accept that time was bleeding her of her beauty?'

Oh, how he must despise her! *Don't rise to it. Fight your corner with pride and with dignity.* Sienna bit her lip as she remembered her mother's pain and—nearly as bad—her worry. 'It certainly wasn't vanity, but neither was it a matter of life or death. Though maybe in a way it was. She needed a hip replacement—she runs a riding school, you see. Without the operation she faced disablement and the closure of her beloved business.'

Sienna looked down and realised that her hands were shaking, but that was nothing compared to the unsteady racing of her heart. She looked again, and this time there was appeal in her green eyes. *Just believe me!* they said. And never had a sense of injustice burned so strong.

'She was at her wits' end, Hashim, and so was I. So I took the easy way out—I admit that. I had once been told that I could make a lot of money—that I wasn't tall enough for the catwalk but that my face and figure could make my fortune. I wasn't at all interested at the time, but I remembered it when I needed to. And I did it. A one-off which I never repeated nor ever would.' She stared at him, braving that dark-eyed look of censure. 'And that's the truth. I swear it.'

There was silence for a moment while he brooded on what she had told him. An interesting development—if it was true. And if it was then perhaps it made her actions slightly less contemptible. But did it actually change anything? Make him forgive her for what she had done?

Never!

In the world Hashim inhabited women were modest and demure, and it was unimaginable to think of them posing naked for money and men's pleasure. He closed his mind as he pictured the calendar as clearly as if someone had just put it down on the table in front of him. Because they weren't just nude shots— no matter how 'artistic' the photographer had tried to make them. She looked…she looked… He felt an involuntary shudder run through his big body and the pooling of lust in his groin.

She looked as if she was begging the viewer to drive himself between her silken thighs!

And no matter what had motivated her it didn't change the fact that she had posed for the erotic shots.

But neither did it change the fact that he wanted her—and he would not rest until he had lost himself in that exquisite body. And only when he had done that, could he cast her aside and forget her.

He was calm again when he spoke. 'And your mother—she approved of your actions? Condoned them, perhaps?'

'Of course she didn't! She didn't know. Not until afterwards.' Sienna shrugged and stared down at the fish congealing on her plate. She wanted to say that she had regretted it bitterly ever since—but that wouldn't be true. She had been glad to help her mother—the only bitterness she had felt was against Hashim, and the way he had made her feel about herself. But even that could not seem to rid her of her longing for him.

Stupid, hopeless longing. How was it possible for this man to deride her, to criticise and pour scorn on her, and yet she was still drawn to that dark, lean body, wanted to see those black eyes soften with passion once more? 'So that's it. Subject closed.' She lifted her eyes and met his stare with a steady gaze. 'So now you know—can we please just forget about this whole farce? You can't possibly want me to work for you—not really. Get someone else to arrange your wretched party for you.'

The corners of his mouth lifted upwards in a cruel imitation of a smile. She still did not get it! Oh, foolish, foolish woman. 'On the contrary, Sienna,' he said softly. 'I do not want anyone else. It is you I want and you that I shall have.'

And Sienna began to tremble.

CHAPTER SIX

A MONTH was no time at all—but in a way Sienna was glad that Hashim had demanded such an outrageously short time to arrange his party. If it had dragged on over weeks, then what kind of state might she have found herself in?

As it was, she had her work cut out to find a venue—and there certainly wasn't time to think about his thinly veiled threat, or the sensual way he had looked at her.

Determinedly, she put him out of her mind and holed herself up in her tiny office at her home in Kennington and rang round, using every contact she'd ever made until at last she struck lucky. She could have the use of Bolland House, set in a hundred acres in the glorious Hampshire countryside. She had driven down to see it and had pronounced it perfect.

She had found a local acclaimed chef who cooked using fresh organic produce sourced from nearby farms. She had chosen flowers, and was bussing in her favourite sommelier—though she had warned him that some of the guests might not be drinking alcohol and asked him to provide a wide selection of soft drinks which were rather more exciting than orange juice!

In fact everything was now in place…and with just three days to go it felt a bit as she imagined the atmosphere in one of the giant space stations just before they sent a rocket into flight—the tension of the countdown was almost unbearable. Especially in this heat.

'I'm making coffee!' called a voice from the kitchen. 'Do you want some?'

'Love some!' Sienna called back, and sat back in her chair and sighed. It was funny how circumstances could change out of all recognition in such a short time. Up until that meeting with Hashim, Sienna had been utterly contented. She had her little terraced house in Kennington, which she had bought as a neglected and nearly derelict wreck. She had spent every spare minute doing it up—stripping the walls, sanding the paintwork and painting it in light colours, filling it with mirrors to make it seem bigger and brighter. She had saved up to have a new bathroom and kitchen put in and had painted the front door in a deep, dark blue.

When the house had been habitable, she had taken in a lodger to help with the mortgage—Kat, who was now in her last year of studying languages at a nearby university. And only then had Sienna given herself the luxury of turning her attention to the garden and the challenge of making something pretty out of the small square of ground which had looked like a builders' yard.

'Coffee's ready!' called Kat.

'Coming!'

Sienna got up and went through to the kitchen, where Kat was just putting the cafetière and mugs onto a pretty spotted tray, her red hair falling over her shoulders. She looked up as Sienna came in and smiled. 'Shall we drink it in the garden?'

'That would be lovely,' said Sienna, but she could hear the flatness in her own voice as she went out into the sunshine.

She felt like an outsider to the rest of the world. Usually she revelled in pride and pleasure at the small oasis she had created in the middle of the city, but not today. She could see the sunlight dappling through the honeysuckle, but she couldn't seem to smell the fragrant blooms, nor appreciate its simple beauty. Hashim's reappearance in her life seemed to have sucked the vibrancy out of everything except the memory of his dark and cruel face, and his hard, virile body.

She took the coffee that Kat poured for her and stared into the cup as gloomily as someone with a fear of heights being told to do a high dive.

'Are you going to tell me what's wrong?' said Kat.

Sienna looked up. Her teeth gritted into the bright, cheery smile which she had become rather good at perfecting. 'Oh, just work. You know. It's frantic at the moment.'

'You don't usually complain,' observed Kat, 'her eyes narrowing. 'You're usually glad when it's like that.'

'Well, it's hot, too. Isn't it?' Sienna wiped her damp brow with a jokey and exaggerated gesture—because how could she tell Kat what was troubling her, and *what* could she tell her?

Oh, I had a fling with a sheikh until he discovered that I'd done some topless photos, and then he…he…

Little beads of sweat studded her forehead and she wiped them away with an angry hand. How awful it sounded when pared down to the basic facts.

She wouldn't tell Kat. Because if she told Kat about Hashim then that would give him an identity which would live on for ever. Kat would want to know all about him—who wouldn't? No, she wouldn't tell anyone. She would do what he wanted her to do and then hopefully he would leave her alone.

Hopefully?

That was part of the trouble, too. He had forced her into this corner and yet a part of her wanted to impress him. To engineer the most wonderful dinner party for him and dazzle him—leaving him with an altogether better memory of her than he currently had.

And wasn't there another part of her—a stubborn and stupid and romantic one—which wished that she could just go back and rewrite history?

Sometimes she started thinking about how it might have been if she'd never done those photos—but then she made herself stop. Thinking like that was a pretty pointless exercise. If she hadn't been able to come up with the money quickly then her mother's life would have collapsed around her—and how could she have lived with *that*?

And even if he hadn't found out it would never have been anything more than a fling—for how could it have been? What had she been imagining—that he'd buy her a whopping great ring and marry her, take her back to Qudamah as the Sheikh's wife? Sienna took a mouthful of too-hot coffee and winced.

'Steady,' warned Kat, only half jokingly.

'Oh, listen—there's that wretched phone again!' Sienna leapt to her feet and gave her housemate an expression which said sorry. But in truth she was glad to get away—to keep herself busy instead of fending off Kat's concerned questions.

'Posh Parties,' she said as she picked the phone up, and then gripped onto it with whitening knuckles.

'Hello, Sienna,' Hashim said softly.

He had the kind of voice which made your skin shiver in spite of yourself, and Sienna closed her eyes in despair. She hadn't spoken to him since that night in the restaurant, and sometimes she had half imagined that she'd dreamt the whole thing up.

But life was rarely as kind as that.

'Hello, Hashim,' she said calmly.

Most people might have asked if it was convenient to talk, but not him.

'It is done?' he questioned, watching as a blonde on the other side of the foyer crossed one slim, silk-stockinged leg over another and slanted him a smile.

'Everything is arranged,' she said mechanically. 'You got my photos of the venue?'

'Yes.'

'And you are happy with the menu plans?'

'Perfectly happy.'

'Drinks seven-thirty to eight, dinner at eight-thirty.' She hesitated. 'Obviously I will be down there earlier, to oversee everything—but do you...do you want me to stay until the end?'

'Most assuredly I do,' he said smoothly, and unseen a slow smile of anticipation curved the cruel line of his mouth. 'And you will dress to party, Sienna. I want you to blend in. Or stand out,' he added mockingly, a jerk of longing arousing him as he imagined her baring her white and perfect breasts. And she would. Oh, she would.... 'The choice is yours.'

She opened her mouth to tell him that she didn't need advice on what to wear—until she realised that antagonising him would get her nowhere. Grit your teeth and bear it, and it will soon all be over.

'I shall look forward to it,' she said crisply.

Hashim's smile became hard-edged. He could see the blonde sliding her tongue wetly over her lips but he turned away. He had never been turned on by the very obvious—and besides, his thoughts were given over to one seduction alone.

'Let's hope it lives up to our expectations,' he murmured, and his black eyes dilated, like a cat's. 'I'll see you on Saturday.' Abruptly he terminated the connection, before the sultry throb of desire could be transmuted to his voice. Because he wanted her to be relaxed, her guard down.

Sienna replaced the phone and stood staring at it for long, countless moments. After Saturday it would all be over.

And suddenly she couldn't wait.

Clunking up the grand drive in her battered old car, Sienna arrived at Bolland Hall just after teatime and let herself in.

'Hello!' she called, but there was no response. She walked through the arched hallway into the dining room and saw the table laid for dinner. She was unable to resist a smile of satisfaction. It was perfect.

Beside Georgian silver and priceless crystal, crisp damask napkins were folded into pristine rectangles and tall candles were ready to be lit.

Everything was as it should be.

There was a stunning floral centrepiece. Fragrant flowers of pink and ivory, dotted with the occasional yellow rose—chosen especially because they were the Sheikh's colours. The colours his jockeys wore. The colour of the Qudamah flag—pink and cream, with a tiny splash of gold in one corner. She breathed in their scent appreciatively.

Similar arrangements of flowers were dotted around the place, and Sienna made her way through the silent house, briefly wondering where all the staff had disappeared to—but they were probably having a well-earned break, since they had clearly been busy.

In the vast kitchen, berry-dark and luscious individual summer puddings lay cooling in the fridge, along with marinades and champagne. Crisp meringues sat snowy-light on a tray next to a bunch of perfect grapes and a dish of white peaches. Several bottles of claret had already been decorked, ready to be carefully poured into the eighteenth-century crystal decanters.

Sienna smiled again. Let Sheikh Hashim Al Aswad try to find any fault with her arrangements!

She heard the crunch of gravel on the drive and wondered if the staff were back. She glanced at her watch. Probably. But as she glanced out of the window she saw a low and screamingly expensive black sports car drawing to a halt. Well, if that was one of the staff then she needed to switch career—and sharpish!

She clip-clopped her way into the hall as the doorbell rang and pulled open the door, her face and her body freezing as she saw Hashim himself standing there, a lazy smile touching the corners of his lips.

Sienna swallowed. She had somehow expected to see him clad in an impeccable dinner jacket, with black tie and snowy white shirt, and dark, tapered trousers which would make his legs look endless. The Western style he seemed to favour the majority of the time.

But he was not. Tonight he was dressed in clothes which heralded far more exotic climes…in fine silk the colour of a pomegranate which clung faintly to hard muscle and lean sinew. It provided the perfect backdrop for his rich black hair and golden-dark skin, but it reminded her of another time—a bitterly erotic one. She felt shame and desire and regret bubbling up inside her, but most of all she felt longing—felt it with an intensity which took her breath away.

Please don't let it show, she prayed silently.

Hashim saw the play of conflicting emotions which crossed her features, and an emotion which was almost alien to him caught him in its silken snare.

Excitement.

'Hello, Sienna.'

'Hashim!' she said softly, in a tone he couldn't quite work out. 'You're…you're early.'

She stood bathed in the soft yet fierce light of the setting sun and he thought that he had never seen her look more beautiful—that thick, shiny hair caught up and woven with glittering clips, making him aware that her neck was classically long and swan-like.

Her dress was made of some light, delicate fabric, layer upon gossamer layer of it, in swirls of rose which made him think of the petals of her mouth. The dress was modest by anyone's standards, even his— and yet he was struck, not for the first time, by how the hint of a body could inflame the senses far more than if it was on show.

As if his senses needed any inflaming!

But he kept his face calmly impassive. This had, after all, been a long time in coming—and he was a master at keeping his feelings hidden. He must not strike until he was certain...

'Aren't you going to invite me in?' he queried mockingly.

She knew she should tell him that it was not her place to invite *him* in—that this was his party, and his money paying for it—but all those thoughts just flew straight out of her mind. For his proximity was making her head spin. She shrank back as he passed by her—as if that could make her immune to the raw virility which seemed to radiate from him. But nothing could make her immune to him.

The black eyes were studying her face as a fox's might just before it devoured a chicken—whole—and a smile was playing around his lips. A smile that made her feel hot and prickly and distinctly...*odd*.

'Do...do you want a drink?' she questioned. 'Or to have a look around—check things out?'

'No.'

She wished he wouldn't stare at her that way, and yet she never wanted him to stop doing it. Pull yourself together, Sienna, she told herself. Remember who he is.

'I'm afraid that the staff have gone off on an extended break,' she said, trying for something light, something to dispel the atmosphere which was fraught and heavy—building into something she didn't recognise nor even want to acknowledge.

And maybe that was why she relaxed and didn't

see it coming. But even if she had would she honestly have been able to stop it? Or *wanted* to stop it?

Because Hashim suddenly pulled her into his arms without warning and anchored her firmly against the full length of his body. His smile hardened.

Don't, she told herself weakly as she felt the musculature and the power. Fight him.

But she did not fight him. She trembled.

And Hashim briefly closed his eyes as one arm encircled the slender column of her waist, sighing with soft triumph as he felt the instinctive flowering of her breasts crushed to his chest. What he had desired for so long would soon be his. It was going to be easier than he had even dared anticipate.

He tilted her chin with the tip of his finger, his black eyes glittering with an inner fire, and she smouldered beneath his scorching gaze. 'Who cares about the staff?' he drawled, and his lips began to move towards her as if a magnetic force compelled them to.

'But—'

'Shh.' His lips grazed hers, touchpaper-sure. 'There are a thousand things I wish to do and show to you, and we must waste not a second.'

Time froze. Her heart seemed to thump out a million beats in those few seconds. His face swam before her, shifting in and out of focus, and she drifted her eyes over it greedily, drinking in the hard, flat planes, the thin, jagged line which ran down the side of his cheek and scarred it.

But most of all it was the mouth which tempted

her—the voluptuous cushion of the lower lip contrasting so markedly with the cruel hard line of the upper one. She could see the gleam of his white teeth and the soft pink of his tongue. It was as if all the time in between had never happened, as if nothing existed nor ever had except for what was here and what was now. In this room, in his arms, in the heightened and fragile atmosphere, with the unsteadiness of their breathing and the scent of the flowers.

'Hashim,' she whispered, but she never knew what it was she intended to say, for his eyes had hardened in tune with his body and he bent his head to blot out the world.

CHAPTER SEVEN

A KISS could be a question and an answer. It could take or give. But Hashim's kiss robbed Sienna of everything except her own helpless response to it. Somewhere at the back of her mind a thousand voices screamed out their protest, but she silenced them as ruthlessly as if they had been her enemies. Instead, she opened her mouth beneath the hard, seeking warmth of his lips. And was lost.

Hashim gave a low laugh of delight at the ease with which she pressed her lips so eagerly against his—it grew in the back of his throat and came out like the small groan of a playful lion cub.

'Oh, yes,' he murmured into her mouth, and she murmured back, something muffled and incoherent—the mindless sound women sometimes made when they were ready for sex.

But Hashim was careful, and although he felt his heart pounding, desire hardening him with its exquisite torturous heat, he knew that this seduction must be a cold-blooded one. One wrong move and she might flee from his arms. One incautious word and all would be lost.

He knew which buttons to press—for his experience of women was encyclopaedic. He knew when to cajole and when to demand. When to lead and when to follow. But with Sienna it was different. She had stated her resistance to just this act, and while her body might be responding at the moment the mind could be a powerful deterrent. Particularly in a woman's case.

It was, he realised, as he drifted his mouth away from her neck and began to kiss softly at the line of her jaw, the very first time in his life that he'd had to actually *seduce* a woman. Normally he had to fight them off. Vaguely he remembered something he had read when schooling himself in the art of love, as royal males of Qudamah did when they reached the age of fifteen. That when a woman was uncertain, you must take it slowly. Very slowly. You must make her believe that you do not have love in mind until it is too late for her to stop. And women did not so easily reach that place of no return as men did.

His mouth was featherlight—provoking and enticing—and Sienna's head fell back. *'Hashim,'* she breathed, and all her hopes and longings were focused on that one little word.

He leapt on the spark of assent and sought to fan the fire with sweet words of his own. 'What is it, sweet Sienna? Sweet, sweet Sienna,' he whispered. His lips touched the base of her throat, teasing it with the tip of his tongue—an erotic and neglected area, or so he had been told—and her little moan told him that his information had been correct. At the same time he began to stroke his fingers down the curve of her hips, taking great care to avoid the obviously erogenous zones. 'That pleases you?'

She felt the pulsing of her blood, felt the words spill from her mouth as if she had no control over them. 'Oh, yes!' she gasped. 'Yes!'

Unseen, he smiled, now risking the flat of his hand lightly skating over her bottom, and in silent answer to the unspoken progression of his movements he felt her squirm against him. The smile disappeared as he let it skate right back again, to cup the pert globe with possessive fingers. Of course she was responsive! Was he forgetting what kind of woman she was? But he dampened his anger down, for it made him harden even more. And it was not his wish to just rip her panties off and drive into her. He would make her eat her defiant words of the other day in the most delicious way possible.

And she would beg him to do it to her!

He teased her and excited her, drifting his fingertips along her thighs, skittering them over the hungry fork of her, but, like a man spoilt for choice at a feast, he deliberately stayed away from her breasts. His mouth hardened. Those he was saving until last.

'Hashim!' she gasped in wonder, as he tiptoed sensation all over her skin, ignited it where he touched, leading her down a path so unbearably sweet that she could scarcely believe this was happening.

His mind worked more quickly than his fingers. If he sought out the classic place of seduction—a bed— then it might allow time for reality to snap into focus and break the spell. He felt himself grow taut, tense, tight, hard as he realised that it was going to have to be here. *Here!* Like a schoolboy with no place to go—but the thought of that, too, excited him. Making do was not something he had ever encountered before, and as always the novel had an intoxicating power all of its own.

When he touched her leg she made no objection. He could feel her impatience and he rewarded it with the slow slide of his hand beneath the filmy layers of her delicate dress, circling the cool satin of her inner thigh to the sound of a tiny moan made at the back of her throat.

'You like that?'

What could she say? Especially as his fingertips were now skating over the moist silk of her panties. Her skin was blazing, her heart was thundering, and warmth and longing overwhelmed her. For only Hashim could make her feel this way—this alive—this wonderful. Like one of those statues brought to life at the end of a play, able to live properly at last. 'Y-yes.' She shuddered. 'You know I do.'

'Then hold me, Sienna,' he urged. 'Hold me.' And as her hands fluttered up to catch hold of the broad bank of his shoulders he gave a grim kind of smile. That was not exactly what he had meant, but for now it would have to do.

Exulting in the freedom of actually touching him again, Sienna was aware that the tips of her fingers were pressing into the fine silk which covered the infinitely finer silk of the skin beneath. Her nails began to scrabble cat-like against the slippery material, as if she wanted to rip it from his body, and he gave a low laugh of delight.

'Ah, yes,' he murmured appreciatively. 'Much better! I see that time has done nothing but hone your appetites.'

His words should have warned her, or stopped her, or cautioned her, but she was in a golden fog of wanting as he began to touch her with a slow, expert caress, and too bewitched to stop him, wanting more, far more.

He pushed aside the damp fabric of her knickers and touched her intimately, where her heat seared against him, and he felt the warmth of her and now he, too, groaned.

'Hashim!' she cried out, startled by sensation—like someone who had jumped out of a parachute after a long absence and forgotten just how mind-blowing it could be. And it had been such a long time...

'You like that?' he teased.

The word was wrenched from her. 'Y-yes.'

'What else do you like?'

'You know,' she breathed. He seemed to know *everything*.

Amid the clamour of his senses he had one last thought of clarity. That the bodyguards stationed at the end of the drive and on the outskirts of the surrounding farmland could not completely guarantee his privacy. Rogue photographers from the hated press might be hiding in the undergrowth—and what a story this would be!

Sheikh caught in flagrante with employee!

Ruthlessly, he continued to move his fingers against her, until, glancing down, he could see that she was lost. Her eyes were smoky and she trembled like a leaf. Was she as receptive as this with every man? he wondered grimly, unprepared for the poisonous snake of jealousy which coiled around his heart. His black eyes scanned the hallway and the dim, dark corridor which ran from the far end of it. Along there they would be unseen.

He felt her stir restlessly and kissed her again, for he knew that a kiss held more power than anything else. That women could be made to fall in love under the spell of a kiss—for they read into it all their secret desires and needs. He felt an infinitesimal moment of hesitation before she melted right into him, and he knew then that her capitulation was certain.

He picked her up in his arms and carried her towards the cool flagstones and the muted colours of a long, silken rug which softened it, lying her down on top of it. Sienna's eyes fluttered open as if she had suddenly just come out of a coma and realised where she was.

'What are you doing?'

There was a strange kind of startlement on her face which almost moved him—until he reminded himself that disingenuous questions like *that* one were sometimes asked out of habit more than necessity. Had she learnt somewhere along the line that men were turned on by innocence? But he would play along with the game if it eased her conscience.

'What do you think I'm doing?' he said softly, as he lay down beside her—*he*, the *Sheikh*, lying on the floor with a woman. 'I am fulfilling my wildest dream and fantasy.'

And hers, too.

'Really?' she questioned tentatively.

'But of course,' he said smoothly, taking her into his arms, knowing that his embrace would dispel any lingering doubts. 'I want you, Sienna. My beautiful Sienna. Indeed, I have never stopped wanting you. Did you not know that?'

She shook her head, her mind a whirl of confusing thoughts. 'But you—'

'Shh.'

His face was close to hers, his breath warm on her face, and all she wanted was for him to kiss her again. She felt the ground hard beneath her back, and the hard body pressing against hers, and fleetingly she wondered how and why she had allowed this to happen. But it was only very fleeting, and suddenly it didn't matter. She couldn't stop. She didn't want to stop.

Once—a long time ago—Hashim had given her a taste of passion and it had branded and spoiled her for ever. The men who had tried to get close to her subsequently had had an impossible act to follow, even if they hadn't been aware of it at the time. And might not this single act help her to exorcise a ghost which was all too real, to move on and break free of his enchantment?

She licked at her dry lips. 'We do not have very long. Wh-what about the staff? The…the guests?' she managed.

Hashim stilled, his eyes narrowing. If there had been any tiny vestige of guilt at his cold-blooded seduction then she had banished it with her words. She knew *exactly* what she was doing. She was sexually hungry, as he was, and probably almost as experienced. Well, then—let her see who was the most magnificent lover of all her conquests!

For he too had been enchanted by the sense of nearly. Of something unfinished and incomplete. In his anger—with himself as well as with her—he had sent her packing before he had properly had his fill of her, and that sense of aching and burning frustration had never quite gone away. Well, now it would—and it would be gone for ever.

'We have long enough,' he said, and the stark note of hunger made his voice sound hollow—as if it came from a long way away—and for a moment he scarcely recognised it as his own.

And hunger made his hands tremble, made his need to join with her overwhelm him with a desire which banished all his carefully conceived plans. Forgotten was his long-nursed wish to feast upon the magnificent breasts which she had displayed for all the world to see. Instead—unbelievably and inexplicably—he found that he didn't want to wait. No—*couldn't* wait.

With a groan, he rucked up her skirt and found himself ripping off the delicate panties. She made no protest, her legs parting for him instantly. His robes were not encumbered by belts or buttons or zips. He could slither off the light silk of his trousers with ease until he was free at last, sliding on the necessary protection with the impatient fumbling of a schoolboy. And then he was touching and nudging against her with a restrained and magnificent power. At last! Such sweet torture, this moment of expectation, but a torture to be treasured and savoured until he could bear it no longer.

'Now,' he whispered—not a question but an emphatic statement, and in answer her lips pressed into his shoulder, opening against him, closing around his flesh. He could feel the wet of her tongue and the sharp graze of her teeth and could contain himself no longer. He drove hard into her.

There was one moment before he realised, a split-second as he worked out what was happening but by then it was too late. He saw the screwing up of her eyes, the way her little white teeth bit down on her bottom lip, and then he knew. By the mountains and the rivers!

'Sienna!' The word was torn from his lips even while her body became taut, like a bow stretched around him, before the arrow of his desire pierced

Play The *Lucky Hearts* Game

and get...
FREE BOOKS & a FREE GIFT...
YOURS to KEEP!

Yes! I have scratched off the silver card. Please send me my **FREE BOOKS** and **FREE MYSTERY GIFT**. I understand that I am under no obligation to purchase any books as explained on the back of this card. I am over 18 years of age.

Scratch Here!
then look below to see what you can claim...

P5II

Mrs/Miss/Ms/Mr _____ Initials _____

BLOCK CAPITALS PLEASE

Surname _____

Address _____

_____

Postcode _____

Twenty-one gets you
4 FREE BOOKS and a
MYSTERY GIFT!

Twenty gets you
1 FREE BOOK and a
MYSTERY GIFT!

Nineteen gets you
1 FREE BOOK!

TRY AGAIN!

The Reader Service™ — Here's how it works:

Accepting your free books places you under no obligation to buy anything. You may keep the books and gift and return the despatch note marked "cancel." If we do not hear from you, about a month later we'll send you 6 brand new books and invoice you just £2.75* each. That's the complete price — there is no extra charge for postage and packing. You may cancel at any time, otherwise every month we'll send you 6 more books, which you may either purchase or return to us — the choice is yours.

*Terms and prices subject to change without notice.

THE READER SERVICE™
FREE BOOK OFFER
FREEPOST CN81
CROYDON
CR9 3WZ

NO STAMP
NECESSARY
IF POSTED IN
THE U.K. OR N.I.

through to the very heart of her. 'Sienna!' he said again, but this time it was on a note of wonder.

'Oh,' she breathed, the word a little feather which drifted away as the pain became transmuted into a growing and indescribable wave of pleasure and he began to move inside her.

He had planned his own release with little concern for hers—not like the first time—but now it was different. Now it was a virtuoso performance. Never had he taken so much care with a woman as he thrust all the way inside her—but then, never had the weight of such responsibility lain so heavy on his shoulders.

He found himself being gentle with her—an odd and unfamiliar kind of gentleness which made what was taking place seem to do so in slow motion, like a film viewed through a gauzy lens.

'Ah, Sienna.' And her name came out on a long, shuddering sigh.

He was slow for as long as he needed to be, and then a little faster. He held back for as long as he needed to, and then he drove in again, harder and then harder still. He teased her when she breathlessly began to beg for more, relentlessly retreating to take her further along the inexorable path, and just when he thought that he could withstand no more of this exquisite self-control he felt her begin to convulse around him.

Her cries split the air, her legs splaying and her back arching as her sweat-sheened face fell back, and she was calling his name in wonder and in disbelief.

And then—oh, sweet, sweet desire—then he let go himself, in an orgasm which rocked his world on its axis—which took him completely out of his body. It was a slow drift back to earth, and he fought it every bit of the way.

It had been the most mind-blowing sex of his entire life—but that should not have surprised him, not really.

After all, he had been waiting for this for a long, long time.

CHAPTER EIGHT

THROUGH the soft darkness Sienna became aware of her heart as it beat within her, strong and loud and steady. And then she became aware of another beat and another heart—so close to hers that it almost felt as if it was inside her. She felt warm and complete—as if she had been made whole at last—the slight aching deep inside her a glorious physical reminder of what had seemed like a perfect dream.

Opening her eyes, she took in the scene with something approaching disbelief. It had not been a dream. She was lying on a carpet in a dim, cool corridor in Hashim's arms, her dress around her hips, and he was staring down at her. Impossible to read what was in those glittering black eyes, but his question gave her some idea.

'Why didn't you tell me?' he asked quietly, his voice as deadly as the silent snakes which glided around the foothills of Qudamah's mountains.

'Tell you what?' she teased.

'Do not play games with me! You are a *virgin*!'

She heard the accusation in his voice and the pink bubble of contentment began to dissolve. 'I was,' she corrected.

He shook his dark head. 'I cannot believe it!'

'I'm afraid you have incontrovertible evidence, Hashim.'

'But...how?'

At any other time his incredulity would have been almost laughable, but now...now it just hurt. 'Surely you don't need me to tell you that?' she questioned quietly.

His mouth tightened. He was still reeling from this one incredible piece of knowledge which had rocked his world just as surely as his orgasm had. For the fact of her innocence had blown all his preconceptions out of the water. And it had done something else, too....

From the start his instinct about her had been that she was innocent, but the existence of the calendar had convinced him that her innocence had been a sham. But if *that* instinct had been correct then what about the other ones which had crowded in on him at the time? The ones which had left him muddled and confused making him wonder if he had found in her something which he had not thought possible?

And hadn't he been glad to abandon those feelings by seizing on her questionable past with something like relief? As if he found it easier to live in a state of cynicism rather than one of hope and longing, like other men.

He shook his head again, dazed and angry, too. 'It should not have been like that.'

She wanted to tell him that it had been perfect, but something in his attitude was puzzling her. He was acting as if something *shameful* had just taken place—rather than the something wonderful it had been. She stared up at him. 'What was wrong with it?'

'Wrong?' A frown creased his brow as he studied her face, rather as a scientist might intently bend over a test tube. 'Nothing was *wrong* with it.' How could she fail to understand? 'But it would never have happened if I had known. Why did you not tell me, Sienna?'

Because she hadn't been thinking of anything except the touch of his lips and the hard, strong embrace of his lean body. She had found it impossible to stop something she had wanted for so long—even though she had denied wanting it. Had told herself that it was wrong to want it.

'We weren't having much of a conversation at the time,' she said, aware that her voice sounded flippant.

'Your first time should not be with a casual lover on the floor of an anonymous house,' he said, and his deep voice was tinged with regret. 'Your virginity is a gift which you have clearly treasured, as every woman should. You should have saved it for a man you love. Who loves you.'

And with those sad words he smashed all her foolish hopes and dreams. He made her feel as if she had offered him fresh flowers at dawn—still wet with the morning dew—and he had taken them and carelessly tossed them into the gutter, to be ground underfoot into dust and crushed petals.

He seemed so far away, even though he was right next to her. A moment ago he had been kissing her over and over again, but he was not kissing her now. The hands which had wrought such sweet magic were not touching her now. It was done. Finished. And Sienna felt the dull ache of dawning realization, which eclipsed the deeper aching in her newly awakened body.

She had allowed…no, she had been a more than willing participant in *allowing* herself to be brought here. To lie with him on this hard stone floor and to…to… She would not use the words 'make love', for it had not been that. It had been nothing to do with love. He had just told her so.

So why were erotic and tender images still jostling for position in her mind? The way she had called out his name in breathless wonder. The way her body had shivered its pleasure, and the way that pleasure had grown and surged and taken her into a place where the senses reigned supreme. And she had stupidly allowed herself to believe that for him it meant more than simply pleasure. That his whispered words of encouragement and pleasure had been voicing some deeper emotion than mere desire—a longing more precious than lust. But in that she had been totally wrong.

Sienna swallowed, forcing the memories away, for they would soon bring nothing but pain. It was too late for regret, but not too late for pride. 'Well, there's no point in having a post mortem, is there?' she said, hearing the false brightness in her tone.

He was silent for a moment, and then his eyes imprisoned her—searching and seeking to know. 'Why has there been nobody else?' he demanded.

It was a question she had asked herself many times—and, oh, how it would feed his monstrous ego if she told him what she suspected was the truth: that he was the only man she had ever remotely imagined making love to. Men had tried, but they had failed. Or was it she who had failed—to abandon foolish hope and try to make the best of an ordinary life?

'You make it sound like a fault on my part that there hasn't been,' she said bitterly.

His eyes narrowed. 'What happened between us that last time. The way I behaved. Did that put you off men?'

'In a way.' But not the way *he* meant.

'You should have told me,' he said, and now his voice was angry. 'Back then you should have told me. But now—*now* when you are older and more independent, a true woman at last—you should have said something!'

'Would you have believed me?'

Another silence.

'Would you?' she persisted.

'No,' he said eventually. 'I guess I wouldn't have.' He felt like a man who had been swimming towards a familiar shore only to discover that he was headed for a strange land of which he knew nothing. None of it made any sense to him. How could it? She? Of all people? A *virgin*?

'Because you'd already made your mind up about what kind of woman I was. The photos proved that I must be some sort of slapper!'

Hashim's eyes narrowed, his English for once deserting him. 'Slapper?'

'The kind of woman who will just sleep with anyone. You didn't look further than skin-deep, did you, Hashim? You just made a judgement about me. But people are a lot more than they appear to be on the surface. Not cardboard cut-outs but living and breathing flesh and blood, with flaws and strengths all their own! Don't you realise that?' she finished.

'I'm afraid that my position sets me apart,' he told her coolly, seeking a familiar refuge behind the invisible barrier of his royal status. 'I do not have the luxury of the time to dig deep beneath the surface.'

'Or the inclination to even try?' she challenged.

'Maybe not,' he admitted, for it was impossible not to answer that lancing question in her green eyes.

Sienna nodded, forcing herself to voice the bitter truth. She had allowed passion to cloud her vision, but now that passion had passed it was achingly clear. 'You see women as commodities,' she whispered. 'To be used for passing pleasure but little else, other than maybe one day motherhood.' And she felt a stupid great yearning as she realised that Hashim would never put her in *that* category. Not in a million years. A woman who had allowed herself to be photographed in that way, a woman who had fallen oh-so-easily into his arms, was merely a woman to be discarded. And the aching sense of longing for something she could never have washed over her in a bitter tide.

He could feel her retreating from him—not just mentally, but physically, too, and that reawakened the desire which had been obscured by his startling discovery. He was used to calling the shots, and by rights *he* should have been the one to distance himself from her now. Or not.

'Ah, Sienna,' he murmured, and reached out his hand to cradle her face. 'What is done is done. Is it not a little late in the day for words of recrimination?'

Involuntarily Sienna trembled—for the touch of his skin was soft and warm and exquisite to behold. It had the power to lure her back into that place of unimaginable pleasure. But at what cost? She shook his hand away and sat up.

'Yes, you're right, it is. I should have said all this before.'

'But you could not!' he breathed triumphantly. 'For you were as much in thrall to me as I to you! What just happened between us was as inevitable as the passing of night through to day. I knew that.'

'Well, we're all entitled to make mistakes,' she said woodenly. 'And anyway, we're wasting time, sitting around here talking. Your guests will be arriving very soon and I suggest that we both of us try to tidy up.' She reached up her hand to feel the bird's nest mess of her hair, wondering how the hell she was going to tame it down.

She was surprised that he wasn't leaping around fretting. He hadn't once mentioned the no-show of the staff. Or the fact that his guests would be upon them shortly. And then something else occurred to her—dripping into her thoughts like slow poison—something which in its way was almost as bad as what she had just let happen. She could feel the heavy plummeting of her heart as everything clicked into disturbingly sharp focus.

Oh, no.

How could she have been so *stupid*?

Slowly, she turned her head to stare at him. 'But there aren't going to be any guests—are there, Hashim?'

He met the accusation in her eyes but he did not flinch from it. 'No.'

'There were never going to be any guests, were there?'

'No.'

She geared herself up for the next blow, knowing the answer to her question before she asked it. 'And the staff? The staff I so carefully vetted and booked but who didn't bother to show?'

'I allowed them to prepare for the dinner, so that your suspicions would not be alerted, and then I cancelled them.'

'You cancelled them,' she said slowly, feeling sickened by the sheer cold-bloodedness of his plan. 'Just like that?'

He shrugged. 'It was not difficult. I paid them in full.'

'*You paid them in full?*' she repeated, her voice shaking, haunted by the thought that she had followed suit. Fallen into line and done exactly what Hashim had wanted. What he had planned. He had lured her into a sensual trap which she had embraced with all the enthusiasm of the convert. She felt the hot sting of hurt but she would not allow it to be converted to tears. She would *not* cry in front of him.

'You snapped your fingers and everybody jumped, I expect. You and your damned money and your damned power,' she whispered. He had tricked her into organising a party just so that he could seduce her—how low could a man sink? And how could she have let him? How *could* she? The true extent of his deception brought fire into her voice.

'You think you can just pick people up and use them, move them around like pawns and then throw them off the board when you've finished with them?' she raged.

Hashim listened, waiting patiently for the storm to pass. Let her rage be spent, and then afterwards let her see sense. Realise that what had passed between them had been magnificent and that to let it go would be a waste of the highest order. Why, he could take her upstairs to one of the magnificent bedrooms, where they could continue to take their pleasure. Her anger would soon be forgotten after a night in his arms!

'Sienna—'

'No!' she said fiercely, pushing away from him and scrambling to her feet. She had seen the brief darkening of his eyes, and she might be new to this game but she knew exactly what it meant. And did she trust herself around him? No, she did not. Her spirit might be fighting all the way, but around Hashim her flesh was as weak as it could be.

She moved as far away from him as possible. There was no dignified way of adjusting her dress and her panties, but she did her damnedest, raking her fingers back through the hair which had tumbled in untidy tendrils all down the side of her long neck.

And at least she had the enjoyment of seeing *Hashim* get to his feet and begin to rearrange his clothing, his face now tight with obvious displeasure and a simmering kind of anger. Or was it merely frustration?

She walked out into the hall, all the warmth and comfort and pleasure evaporating from her body like raindrops on a scorching pavement. And then she caught a glimpse of herself in the mirror and recoiled at the sight of her flushed cheeks and mussed hair— the definite look of someone who had been rolling around the place.

How could she? Oh, how *could* she?

She picked up her handbag and a silken voice stopped her in her tracks.

'Where do you think you are going?' he questioned softly.

Composing her face, she turned round, and suddenly she didn't care *what* he tried to threaten her with. Just let him try. Nothing could be worse than what she had just allowed to happen, despite all her supposedly good intentions. 'Home,' she said crisply. 'Where else?'

'You could come home with me.'

Sienna almost choked. 'I'd rather spend the night in a lions' cage! And anyway—I wouldn't call a luxury hotel suite a *home*! It isn't yours, it's anonymous—just like this place. There's nothing of you there, Hashim. A luxurious room with no soul. And that's your life. Empty.'

For a moment a dark shadow passed across his heart. She dared to say this to him? To accuse him of an empty life? He, who had palaces and oil fields and people scattered all over the world who were eager to do his bidding? No woman had ever dared say such a thing to him. She was daring to look at him and speak to him as no woman ever had before...almost as his *equal*. Again he felt the sensation of being on unfamiliar territory, and his mouth hardened in anger.

'I forbid you to go!'

'Well, you can't. You don't own me. You don't even employ me any more. I've done what you asked and now I'm leaving.'

His eyes narrowed as he glanced around the carved

wooden interior of the airy hall. 'And what of this house and your obligation to it?' he demanded.

'It's not my concern. Not any more. *You* sort it out! Here!' And she flung the keys at him.

He caught them one-handed, realising that she meant exactly what she said. She was leaving! Walking out on him even though she had been sobbing out his name only moments before. And suddenly he was filled with a reluctant kind of admiration which only renewed the subtle throbbing of desire. 'Has anyone ever told you how beautiful you look when you're angry?' he questioned softly.

'Fortunately, most people have a more original line than that!'

'But it is not finished yet, Sienna,' he said evenly. 'I tell you that quite unequivocally. You have but tasted the pleasures I can give you, and soon you will be greedy for more.'

'Oh, but you're wrong. So wrong.' She stared at him. 'After all, we're even now. I deceived you, and now you've paid me back by deceiving me. We can call it quits. I just want to forget you and your fake party. In fact, I want to forget all about you.'

He shook his head and his mouth curved into a cruel smile. 'You still don't understand, do you, Sienna? Those are not *my* wishes—and the Sheikh always has *his* wishes fulfilled.'

He wasn't listening to a word she said! Frustratedly, she turned away, and his dark laughter was still ringing in her ears as she slammed her way out of the front door, running down to where her beaten-up little wreck of a car was parked beside his smooth, dark sports model. And if she needed some concrete evidence of the insurmountable differences in their lives she had only to look at their two contrasting cars.

It's over, she told herself fiercely.

So why did she look up into the driver's mirror to see his tall dark figure, the silken pomegranate robes whispered by the breeze to caress that hard, honed body which had made such sweet and unforgettable love to her?

She turned the key in the ignition with an angry jerk. It was over.

CHAPTER NINE

HASHIM rang her. Repeatedly. Sienna kept the phone on 'divert', but once she picked it up without checking and heard his voice, and quietly terminated the connection with a trembling hand.

He sent her a cheque—such a grossly inflated cheque that the businesswoman side of her momentarily weakened, until she allowed her righteous fury to put it in an envelope and send it back to him. She supposed she could have torn it up—but returning it might help to get the message through loud and clear.

He even tried flowers—and for some reason those riled her more than anything. How *dared* he think he could buy her off with a bunch of flowers?

'They're lovely,' Kat said wistfully, sniffing at the lily-of-the-valley and freesia and roses.

'Have them—they're yours!' And Sienna unceremoniously dumped the monster bouquet into her bemused lodger's arms.

Her work, which had previously fulfilled her, suddenly seemed a chore, and her life felt like a punctured balloon, coloured grey. Kat had taken to asking if she was sickening for something, and Sienna knew that she really was going to have to snap out of it. She had a business to run and she couldn't divert her phone for ever. And Hashim seemed to have got the message at last, since he had left her alone for nearly a week.

She was sitting in her minuscule office, trying to concentrate on an engagement party which seemed to mock her with its celebration of love, when the telephone on her desk rang. Tiny hairs on the back of her neck began to prickle as she heard a disturbingly familiar dark, silken voice, and she wavered for a second. She could hang up, of course—or she could have the courage to tell him to leave her alone. And she couldn't keep running away for ever.

'What can I do for you, Hashim?' she questioned coolly.

'Why have you failed to cash my cheque?' he demanded.

'Because I don't want your money!'

'Ah, Sienna,' he purred, like a trainee lion cub. 'Don't you realise that resistance turns a man on?'

Especially a man who wasn't used to being resisted. 'That isn't why I'm doing it,' came her icy reply.

He knew that. As a ploy it would have failed, because he would have seen through it. As a genuine wish it excited him. Greatly. 'I want to see you,' he said softly.

Images of his dark mocking eyes swam into her unwilling memory. 'Well, you can't.'

Did she not realise that he could hear her breathless note of hesitation—and the reluctant longing which matched his own? His voice dipped into a mocking caress as he felt the hot, hard jerk of desire. 'Then say it like you mean it.'

Sienna closed her eyes, but that only made it worse. Now the images were of a hard body entering hers with almost heartbreaking sweetness. 'There's no point,' she said wildly.

'On the contrary. There is every point. I have a proposition to put to you.'

'A proposition?' Suspicion crept into her voice. 'Planning another fictitious party, are you?'

He gave a low laugh. 'Now, that's an idea! Meet me and I'll tell you all about it.'

'Have you listened to a word I've been saying? I don't want your phone calls or your flowers, and I certainly don't want to *see* you, Hashim!'

'Yes, you do,' he murmured. 'You know that and I know that. You are unsettled and so am I. Why keep fighting it? Your work will suffer, for a start.'

And he was right, damn him! She had almost more work than she could reasonably cope with, and—ironically—no inclination to do it. It had taken every bit of concentration she had to prevent herself from sitting staring into space and thinking about the dark Sheikh, trying to school herself away from wanting him, but in reality… Oh, the reality was so different.

'If I meet you, will you promise to leave me alone?'

He gave a wry smile. How had she managed to get

so far with such an appalling sense of logic? 'If that is what you desire,' he said carefully.

Desire. What a dangerous and provocative word that was. Sienna clenched her fist as she felt the empty little tug of her heart. 'Name a time and place.'

'Now.'

'*Now?*'

'I am very close to your house. I will be waiting.'

'You *are* joking!'

'What's the matter, Sienna?' he mocked. 'Are you never spontaneous?'

She was wearing her oldest jeans and a T-shirt which one of the football team had given her at college. There was a rip at the hem and a stain on it which she thought might be *crème de menthe*, but she wasn't entirely sure. She glanced in the mirror at her unwashed hair, which was caught back in a ponytail. Maybe if he saw her like this—the real, basic Sienna—then he would get the message.

'Okay,' she said slowly. 'I'll meet you.'

'Five minutes,' he clipped, and hung up.

Pausing only to brush her teeth, telling herself that she would have done the same no matter who she was meeting, she slid on a pair of old flip-flops and let herself out of the house, wondering where he was waiting.

She didn't have to wonder for very long. A shiny limousine with tinted windows was parked at the end of the road—presumably because the road was so narrow it could go no further. In front of it and just to the rear were two leather-clad outriders on powerful motorbikes. It was like a scene straight out of a film, and Sienna could see a couple of curtains twitching as she walked towards it.

My neighbours will never look at me in quite the same way she thought, as a chauffeur stepped out of the driver's seat and opened the door for her.

Telling herself that she could hardly be rude to Hashim's employee, she had no choice but to slide into the soft-cushioned luxury of the back seat. It took a few seconds for her eyes to become accustomed to the dim light, but she could see Hashim sprawled negligently on the back seat, watching her.

Today he was wearing Western clothes—not a shimmer of soft silk in sight. An immaculately cut dark suit, with a snowy shirt and a tie which gleamed dully in the reduced light. Sienna could feel her heart begin to pound.

'Nice of you to get out of the car yourself,' she said.

'I was thinking of your reputation.'

'Liar.'

He laughed. 'Your assessment of me is wholly and completely wrong, Sienna—my honesty has at times been described as almost brutal.'

Brutal. Yes. There *was* a brutal side to his nature. And yet it contrasted with the extraordinary gentleness he had displayed when she had lain so helplessly in his arms. She felt the drying of her lips, and as if he had read her thoughts he leaned forward and touched his mouth to hers in a barely-there kiss which started her senses sizzling.

'Don't,' she said weakly.

The same cold skill and calculation which made him a world-class poker player made him kiss her for long enough to hear her sigh, and then he stopped and leaned back against the seat to study her. He pressed a button by his side and said something she did not understand. The car began its powerful acceleration.

'Where are we going?' she questioned, in alarm.

'Just driving around—we will draw less attention to ourselves that way—this car tends to attract sightseers.'

'Why don't you travel in something less ostentatious, then?' she questioned acidly.

'Because I cannot,' he said simply. 'It needs to be bullet-proof.'

And—perhaps for the very first time—Sienna allowed herself to see the downside of his life. Hadn't there been part of her which had somehow thought that the bodyguards which accompanied him were simply for show? As some kind of indicator of his power and lofty position? She had never actually stopped to think that someone might want to *shoot* him, and now that she had she found her stomach twisting over in anxiety.

'Now, let us both be honest,' he said quietly. 'Can you do that?'

'You don't take any notice of me when I am.'

But he shook his head. 'No, Sienna—I am talking about *real* honesty. I do not mean that you should say what you feel you *ought* to say, but what is truly in your heart.'

'Then I'm at a disadvantage—for *you* don't have a heart!'

He paused, for it was not the first time this accusation had been flung at him. 'Have you thought of me?'

She opened her mouth to say no—but something in his eyes stopped her. 'Yes.'

He nodded his head. 'And for me it is the same. I have thought of little else. The way you felt in my arms. You haunt me, Sienna—for I cannot forget the great gift which you gave to me.'

'Which you took, you mean,' she corrected him quietly. 'You set me up and seduced me—as you had intended to do right from the start.'

'Yes,' he said bitterly. 'Of that I am guilty—I robbed you of your greatest virtue. But I would not have done it had I known that you were innocent, and that innocence has changed everything.' He paused, studying the lush fullness of her mouth, and when he spoke his voice was almost reflective. 'What passed between us was not enough—not for me, nor for you. You were beautiful and responsive, but your initiation into the pleasures of the body should not be limited to a single session on a cold floor, our bodies not even naked.'

She was glad then for the dim light, for she began

to blush and he saw. His eyes narrowed and she wondered if he was remembering—as she was—that very first blush such a long time ago. 'It's over,' she said, aware of how lacking in conviction her words sounded. Was that because she didn't *want* it to be over?

He thought how strange it was that a woman could still blush with innocence, even when that innocence was gone. 'Ah, but that is where you are wrong,' he whispered. 'It is not over. Indeed, that was only the beginning.'

Sienna blinked, because suddenly the picture had shifted, changed focus. Was he asking her to be his *girlfriend*? 'What are you saying?' she whispered.

'You came to me untutored—a beautiful novice,' he said huskily. 'And yet, in a way, it was as new for me as it was for you.' His black eyes glittered. 'You see, I had never had a virgin before.'

He made himself sound like a jockey who had attempted a higher than usual jump, and his matter-of-fact words fractured the tiny flicker of hope which had begun to spark into life. But maybe that was a blessing, because the very word 'virgin' was charged with emotion—and emotion could, she realized, be character-changing in every sense of the word. It could make you weak when you most needed to be strong. 'Am I supposed to be flattered by this remarkable statement?'

'Yes,' he said simply. 'For I am admitting to you that I found the experience profoundly moving.'

As an admission it bordered on the arrogant, and if it had been anyone else then Sienna might have said so. But something stopped her. Maybe it was the look in his eyes. As if he had lifted away a veil and allowed her to see a whisper of contrition. And the unexpected glimpse of this gave him the fleeting shimmer of vulnerability, reminding her that deep down he was just a man—that all the rest was just packaging.

'Go on,' she said steadily. 'I'm intrigued.'

'I want to teach you everything there is to know about the art of love.' His smile was edged with hunger. There was the briefest of pauses before he spoke again. 'I want you to become my mistress,' he said softly.

Sienna stilled. *'What?'*

'I am choosing you to become mistress to the Sheikh.'

He made it sound so...*mechanical.* 'Is there a new vacancy, then?' she questioned acidly. 'Or will I be sharing the post?'

Hashim was so used to complete compliance—to grateful and eager acceptance from adoring women—that for a moment he was taken aback by her flippant attitude. 'I do not think you realise the honour I am affording you,' he said icily.

'No, I probably don't,' said Sienna gravely. 'Perhaps you could tell me a little more about what this exciting position entails?'

Because no one ever made fun of him Hashim did

not recognise the mocking tone in her voice. He had never had to persuade or to entice a lover before, and such coercion did not come naturally to him.

'You will have an open charge account.' His black eyes flicked disparagingly over her jeans and stained T-shirt. 'And in future you will buy clothes that please you and please your Sheikh.'

'Do you have any particular requests?' Sienna questioned meekly. 'Favourite colours? That kind of thing?'

Hashim's eyes narrowed suspiciously. Was she agreeing without further argument? Damn the woman—why did she keep coming out and surprising him? 'Obviously what you are wearing today is thoroughly unsuitable.'

'Obviously,' she agreed steadily.

'I should like to see you in silks and satins from now on,' he said coolly. 'And velvets and lace. Nothing *man-made*.' He shuddered. 'You should dress to please me, for when I am pleased then it follows that you shall be, too.'

'How delightfully simple you make it sound,' Sienna murmured. 'Anything else?'

His black eyes gleamed with anticipation as he imagined clothing her in delicate underclothes—and then ripping them off! 'As you know, I spend the majority of my time in Qudamah, but I frequently travel to the major cities to conduct business on behalf of my country, and when I do I wish for you to fly out to join me. I will send my private jet for you,' he promised silkily.

She ignored the airborne carrot he dangled. 'But what about my job?' she questioned seriously.

'Your job?'

'Or rather, my career,' she corrected. 'I've built it up from scratch and worked hard—I can't just abandon it to flit off to all the corners of the globe on a whim.'

Hashim gave her an impatient look. 'Your job will no longer be necessary. You will have all the money you need. You can give it up.'

Give it up? Sienna could not hold her feelings in any more. Did he have no idea how real people lived their lives? She supposed that he didn't. 'I'm not doing any such thing!' she declared. 'I take pride in my work, Hashim. I have a number of big contracts in the pipeline.'

'Sub-contract them.'

'No, I will not.'

'Sienna, you are stretching my patience!'

'And you're stretching mine! Do you imagine for a moment that I can be bought?'

There was a moment of silence. 'Everyone can be bought—you of all people should know that.'

'Are you still on about those wretched photographs? Can't you just let it go?' She stared at him and then reached for the door. 'I won't be insulted by you any more. And I don't have to be. You've had your pound of flesh, Hashim—just be satisfied with that.'

Suddenly he found himself wishing that he could bite the words back. 'Sienna. Don't go.' He caught her arm and began to caress it with his fingers. 'Please.'

She closed her eyes, her inner turmoil lulled by the touch of his hand, recognising that his plea was an unfamiliar one. She had made her stand and demonstrated her independence and her pride—but nothing could change the effect he had always had on her, and still did. The melting way he made her feel inside whenever he touched her. The way his very presence made her feel so *alive*. If she took that out of the equation there would be nothing to consider, but it was far too powerful to disregard.

She opened her eyes again. 'It's not all about what *you* want, is it, Hashim? It's about what I want, too.'

He had been almost certain that she was—incredibly!—going to turn him down, and it was Hashim's turn to be surprised. Was she playing games with him? 'You mean you are giving consideration to my proposal?'

'Of course I am. A woman would have to be pretty stupid not to, wouldn't she? It isn't every day that she is offered a chance to play the starring role in Cinderella!'

But, inexplicably, his triumph was now tempered by a fleeting sense of disappointment—for it now appeared that she was going to give in, and he had been enjoying doing battle with her. 'So you will agree?'

'Only if you agree to my terms.'

'*Your* terms?' he repeated, outraged.

'But of course. Why should it all go your way?'

Because it always had done—all his life! 'Name them,' he snapped.

'Well, you can forget the idea of a charge card, for a start—I don't want it, thank you all the same. I don't earn a fortune, but what I do has been honestly come by—and I usually manage to scrub up well enough without the benefit of costly clothes. And I will only fly to see you if it is convenient. To me.' Because soon it would be over, and when it was she would need her livelihood just the same as she always had. 'I will continue with my life as normal—if you want to see me then you will have to fit in around me.'

'But what you ask of me is outrageous!' he protested.

She shrugged. 'Then forget the whole idea. In fact,' she added truthfully, 'that would be much better for me in the long-term.'

'But in the short-term you do not want to forget it,' he murmured, pulling her into his arms. 'Right now your body is screaming out for me. You know that I am growing hard even now, just as you are wet with wanting. Aren't you?'

'Hashim, you're…you're…' But her words were forgotten, for he had put his hands underneath her T-shirt to cup the aching mounds of her breasts.

'No bra?' he questioned shakily, torn between excitement and disapproval as he felt their velvet weight against his palms.

'I never wear one when I'm working at home. Oh!' She gasped as he bent his mouth to one hardened nipple and began to suckle it. His hand was skimming the narrow indentation of her waist, which led down to an unforgiving waistband. And now his hand had moved to the fork of her thighs, and he was touching her through the denim...touching her and touching her. 'Hashim, wh—what do you think you're doing?'

'Guess.'

'But...but we're in the car.'

'The driver can't see. Do you want me to stop?'

She squirmed with pleasure beneath his touch. Not yet. Just a couple of minutes more and then she would stop him. 'We can't actually *do* anything if I'm wearing jeans, can we?' she asked breathlessly.

'Can't we?' He laughed, skating a featherlight fingertip over the most intimate part of her.

How could she feel this way? As though he was touching her flesh instead of the thick material of her jeans. 'Hashim—'

'Shh. Let go,' he urged, excited now as he watched her. 'Just let go.'

And to her eternal shame she did just that. Forgot the fact that she was writhing around in the back of a car in the middle of heaven only knew where. Forgot that she might have salvaged a little pride by returning his cheque and refusing his calls. She just went right along with the demands of her body, allowing herself to be carried along by the sweet and irresistible torrent.

'Oh!' She half sobbed as he increased the movement of his finger.

'Yes,' he murmured. 'You are so close, Sienna. So beautifully close. Let me watch you as I give you pleasure. Let me see you orgasm in your blue jeans.'

And then that feeling was upon her again—that out-of-this-world, flying-to-paradise feeling was sweeping her up and away, orchestrated by the relentless and expert caress of his fingers. And suddenly she had begun to cry out—little cries of astounded pleasure—until the fierce pressure of his mouth blocked out the sound and her body shattered into a million beautiful pieces.

For countless seconds she felt the spasms of her body shuddering to a slow halt, the sticky warmth of contentment. She was aware of Hashim stroking away the hair from her sweat-sheened brow.

'How can that have happened?' she whispered, half to herself. 'How?'

Unseen, he smiled. How little she knew—and how much he had to show her! He lifted her chin so that he could stare down at her with black eyes which mocked and lanced. 'Ah, Sienna,' he said softly. 'Do you see how much you have to learn?'

Lying curled in his arms in the aftermath of her orgasm, she was at her most vulnerable. 'Perhaps I do,' she agreed drowsily.

Maybe when you first gave your heart to someone it was difficult to claw it back again. With Hashim there had always been a sense of something left uncompleted—hadn't he said so himself? Maybe this really was the answer. If she saw more of him then mightn't it diminish some of the magic which surrounded him? Which made her see him as she failed to see other men?

'So you will agree to be my mistress?'

She turned her face up to his and opened her eyes very wide. 'Only on a strictly informal basis.'

'And will you come back to my hotel now and let me give you dinner?'

And, presumably, bed. But that was what a mistress *should* do—and who was she to complain if it meant that Hashim would make love to her?

'I'll need to go home and get showered first.'

He gave a slow smile of anticipation. 'We'll have a bath together,' he said. And he would send out those disgusting clothes of hers to be laundered.

CHAPTER TEN

Six months later

'YOU are late,' Hashim said coldly, as Sienna walked into the hotel bedroom.

'Only a little.'

'I have been waiting,' he said ominously, 'for over an hour.'

'Sorry, darling.' Sienna slipped off the soft green cashmere coat she had allowed him to buy her for Christmas, its emerald *faux* fur collar gleaming in the pale winter sunshine. It was the *only* thing she had allowed him to buy—and then only because it was Christmas. Even though—as she had teasingly pointed out—he didn't actually *celebrate* Christmas.

'But *you* do!' he had growled.

In a way, it frustrated him that she had steadfastly refused to be showered with the gifts which he thought were her due—but then, he didn't have a monopoly on frustration. She had discovered early on that it went hand-in-hand with the pleasures of being a mistress.

It was such an unreal existence.

So many of their meetings were conducted in secret—behind the closed doors of hotel rooms—while they lost themselves in each other's arms. Sometimes they would slip out to a discreet restaurant for a meal—though always shadowed by the ever-present bodyguards.

It was easier in Paris or some of the Spanish cities—which afforded more anonymity—but being abroad only increased Sienna's sense of unreality. The certainty that this relationship could not last, and her fear of when it would end. Whether it would be less painful if it happened sooner rather than later.

It was as though what they had between them was so fragile that any kind of analysis might shatter it. And it wasn't even something she could talk to her girlfriends about—and certainly not her mother. When you had an ordinary relationship—were having those ordinary fears about where it was headed—then friendly advice was yours for the taking.

But being a mistress was an indeterminate occupation, frowned on by society in general—both his *and* hers. For it flew in the face of the family values which most people believed in, deep down.

Only in her case she was not strictly a mistress. Hashim didn't have a wife waiting at home. Instead he had a country—which was far more demanding.

She turned to watch him as he pressed a button on the wall and the heavy drapes slid silently to a close, blocking out the daylight and enclosing them in their own private world.

Hand provocatively placed on her hip, Sienna raised her eyebrows as he turned round. 'You complain that I've kept you waiting, and yet you haven't even kissed me hello yet!'

Exasperated and turned on, he pulled her into his arms and kissed her. 'Hello.'

'And hello to you, too.'

He rubbed his forehead against hers. 'How you love to make me angry, Sienna.'

'No, I don't,' she said seriously. 'It's just that you work yourself up into a complete state when I don't do exactly what you say.'

'But you never do what I say.'

'Ask me something—anything—and I will!'

He took her face between his hands and looked down at her. 'Will you kiss me again, my non-compliant and informal little mistress?'

She lifted her lips to his, winding her arms around his neck, giving a little yelp of pleasure as their mouths collided in a kiss which this time was much more than a greeting. It was a hard, hungry and frustrated kiss. She hadn't seen him in nearly a month, and he wasn't supposed to be here for another fortnight.

But he had sandwiched in an extra trip to London on the way back from the States and called her at the last minute. Sienna had decided not to play games for the sake of it and had agreed to change her diary around. And bought a new set of underwear.

In between the frantic unzipping and unbuttoning of their clothes there were fractured bursts of conversation.

'I've missed you,' he groaned.

'Good.'

He reached down and slid off first one high-heeled shoe and then the other, caressing a silk-clad ankle on the way. 'You're supposed to tell me that you missed me, too.'

'That...oh!' She shivered as he rippled his fingers up over a stocking-top and circled the satin flesh above it. 'That is what I would call fishing for a compliment.' She gulped.

His hand halted. 'So you didn't?'

'You've only been gone a month.'

'*Only?*' he questioned ominously.

She reached down and guided his hand back again. 'Yes, yes, yes—I've missed you. I've thought about you constantly and dreamt of this moment! Is that better?'

'Much better,' he murmured. 'If it is true.'

Oh, yes, it was true, she thought as he carried her over to the bed and put her down in the centre of it. She had missed him more than he would ever know and more than she would ever tell him. She might have been a novice when she started her affair with Hashim—but she was growing to learn the rules. And the number one rule seemed to be always keep something back.

She had recognised early on that her Sheikh was a natural hunter—and that like all hunters he enjoyed the thrill of the chase. He was never more passionate than when she didn't leap into line. It wasn't the hardest psychology in the world to work out that a man for whom the world jumped would be fascinated by someone who didn't.

And for Sienna it was less about game-playing than protecting herself. Stopping herself falling deeper in love with a man who could never reciprocate the emotion. But holding back love wasn't as easy as playing hard to get. Love was like sunlight outside the dark of a barn—there were always cracks and crevices for it to come flooding inside.

She pushed the thoughts away as he took off her dress, her bra and her panties—though he left her stockings and suspender belt on. Lying back against the cushions, she watched as he removed his clothes, peeling off his suit and shirt and skimming off his silken underwear until he was formidably and powerfully naked.

Sometimes she touched herself while he undressed, as he had taught her to—rubbing at her breasts or teasing him with the tantalising stroke of a finger between her legs. Sometimes he even liked to watch her bring herself to orgasm—but today she could see a tight tension in his muscular body, and she frowned and did not tease him.

When he came to lie beside her she noticed the dark shadows beneath his eyes and lifted a finger to touch them. 'You're tired,' she observed softly.

'Then make me untired.'

'Is there such a word as untired?'

'There is now.' He closed his eyes as she licked

with her tongue from nipple to belly and then beyond, to where he was unbearably hard. 'Ah, Sienna,' he groaned. 'Where the hell did you learn to do that?'

'You taught me, Hashim,' she murmured, before taking him slowly into her mouth. 'Remember? You taught me everything.'

Afterwards he thought that he had taught her perhaps too well... She was like a whore in the bedroom—as a woman should be. She was everything he had ever dreamed of—and more. And one day another man would benefit from his tutition—perhaps sooner than either of them had anticipated. Another man would see her head bobbing up and down on his lap, her mouth working sweet spells while she took him to paradise and back. His lips twisted as a sting of pain caught him unawares, but then fatigue wrapped him in its gritty arms and he slept.

When he awoke it was to see Sienna lying propped on one elbow watching him, her hair spilling down all over the rosy flush of her breasts, and in that hazy moment between sleep and waking he gave an instinctive smile—for this was the place in which he most liked to find himself.

She thought that he looked like a lion who had temporarily sated his huge appetite. A fleeting look of contentment before the relentless and ruthless search for sustenance once more. He drove himself, she had realized, more than most men would even be capable of doing. And, whilst he had a huge capacity for hard work and long hours, she had never seen that weary tinge to his smile before.

She touched his lips with a gentle finger. 'So, is it jet-lag?'

'Maybe.' He kissed the finger. She was so easy. So perceptive. Sometimes it was hard not to tell her the things on his mind, but he rarely gave voice to his innermost thoughts. For a ruler it was preferable to keep your own counsel, but sometimes—in the aftermath of making love to Sienna—he found himself wanting to offload his problems, as other men apparently did. He wondered what had changed, and when it had happened.

Something had crept up on him unawares. Maybe it was like the shadow on your jaw. You didn't notice it—and it wasn't until your chin was grazed with the dark rasp of stubble that you remembered it was well on its way to becoming a beard.

Sienna brushed away a lock of the dark hair which had tumbled onto his forehead. Against the white sheets his body looked so golden and erotically dark—like a rich oil painting brought into vibrant and glowing life before her eyes. 'You don't usually suffer from jet-lag,' she observed quietly.

'No.'

There was silence for a moment, and Sienna knew that she could do one of two things: she could get up and go into the plush kitchen of the hotel suite and make them both a cup of the iced jasmine tea he so loved and which she had learned to love, too. She could put on soft and soothing music and run him a deep, deep bath and then join him in it. And later they would make love again. And again. That was what a mistress would and should do.

Or she could venture onto the always precarious path of finding out just what was going on in that clever, quick mind of his. Six months ago she wouldn't have dreamed of contemplating it—but hadn't Hashim been softer of late? Didn't the enigmatic and formidable side of his nature sometimes seem less dominant, so that sometimes he seemed much more *accessible*?

'So, do you want to tell me what's wrong, or do you want me to run away and do womanly things?'

'Like what?'

'Oh, you know…tea, a bath, music.'

A smile edged the hardness away from his mouth. 'No, don't go. Stay here. You've just done the most important thing a woman can do for a man.'

There was another silence, and Sienna tried hard not to read too much into his words. Just because he had sounded uncharacteristically tender it did not mean anything. He was basically applauding her rapidly improving skills as a lover and thus his own skills as an expert tutor—that was all. Or he was being slightly more affectionate because they hadn't seen each other for a few weeks. There were any number of reasons.

But the shadows were still beneath his eyes; the weariness still outlined his mouth. She thought about what he had taught her, and about her refusal to just jump when he snapped his fingers. Hashim respected that, she knew. What he would not countenance was fear or timidity.

'Are you going to tell me what's wrong?'

He shifted position a little, so that he was lying gazing into the huge green glitter of her almond-shaped eyes. The breasts he had once been so obsessed with now seemed just a part of the beautiful whole of her, but still their pert rosiness reminded him of how she had used them, how that could never be undone—at least not for him.

'Just tired. It's nothing,' he murmured—which was true, though only part of the story. There was growing opposition in Qudamah to his Western lifestyle—a demand from some factions that he settle down and embrace completely the culture of his ancestors. There had been views expressed that his trips abroad should be curtailed, with all his energies focused on his homeland.

And didn't Sienna herself exemplify everything that the more traditional elements in his country loathed about the West? Hadn't Abdul-Aziz increasingly been hinting that the liaison was damaging his credibility? That things would blow up if some resolution were not reached? And Hashim knew what that resolution should be.

'It's nothing,' he repeated firmly.

Sienna did her best not to let her face crumple with disappointment. She had asked him and he had closed up—she could tell from the shuttering of his face. Well, that was up to him. It had been her choice to ask and his not to tell her. Asking was one thing, and perfectly acceptable. Prying was something completely different.

She took his words at face value, as he clearly wanted her to. 'So, when did you last have a holiday?'

'A holiday?' he questioned, as surprised by the choice of topic as by her sudden change of subject.

She laughed, pleased to have perplexed him. 'Yes, a holiday. That's the thing that most people do when they're tired and they want to relax.'

He screwed up his eyes. 'I don't remember,' he said.

'No recent bucket and spade job in Spain?' she teased.

'Bucket and spade job?' He frowned.

'Have you never built sandcastles, Hashim?' she questioned.

He laughed. 'Sand is not a big deal in Qudamah— not with so much of it around. We tend to escape from it rather than build our leisure time around it,' he added drily.

'I'd never thought of that.' She snuggled up to him. 'So what kind of holidays did you have when you were a child?'

He frowned. 'You don't really want to know.'

Which meant he didn't really want to tell her. But a woman could not exist on sex alone, no matter what her status. 'Oh, yes, I do!' she said firmly.

And Hashim found himself smiling as he allowed himself a rare dip into nostalgia. How long ago a childhood could seem, and yet how astonishingly clear the memories if you opened the floodgates on them. 'My male kin and I used to take our falcons up into the forests, where we trained them to kill.'

'Nice!'

Idly, he circled the pad of his finger around one of her nipples, feeling it instantly point and peak, and he felt the heavy stir of desire returning. 'There we learned to be men,' he said dreamily.

'No women?'

'Not one.'

'But what about your mother? Didn't she want to go along?'

He remembered the very first trip, being torn from his mother's arms. He had been just five years old and had cried his eyes out. How remorselessly the others had teased him! And his father had told him that the painful separation was all part of the process of learning to be a man. He could imagine what a Western psychologist would say about *that*!

'Females were not part of the endeavour,' he said thoughtfully. 'Their place was at the Palace.'

'And didn't they mind?'

He hesitated. 'My mother *did* mind, as it happens,' he admitted. 'And she made vocal her concerns. It caused a great deal of conflict between her and my father—but she was determined that the women of Qudamah should make some of the changes which women over the world were initiating at the time. Nothing like burning their bras, of course,' he added hastily.

Sienna laughed. 'Well, no.'

'But through her efforts the women of Qudamah were gradually granted small freedoms.'

'Such as?'

He shrugged. 'Oh, they were allowed to walk in the capital unaccompanied by a man—though many still prefer not to.' He saw her face. 'To you this probably means nothing—a woman who has grown up with personal freedom and takes it for granted probably cannot comprehend that in my country it was a kind of revolution.'

'She sounds like an amazing woman,' she said.

'She is.' The words *I should like you to meet her* hung unsaid on the air. For, no matter how true they were, how could he possibly utter them in the circumstances?

Sienna was quiet for a moment. She had heard the deliberate omission and she wouldn't have been human if it hadn't hurt her. What a different world he painted, and how his words emphasised the huge gulf between their cultures. If she had never understood his extreme reaction to her calendar shoot she certainly did now. If it was considered a mighty advance for a woman to go out on her own, then how must the baring of her breasts for an erotic calendar have seemed to a man of such a traditional upbringing?

But if ever she succumbed to the hopeless temptation of thinking *what if*—then all she had to do was remind herself of the insurmountable differences which had always been there and always would. No matter what they did—it was *doomed*.

And Sienna had realised something else, too—Hashim might have been bordering on the brink of love all those years ago, but his feelings—and hers—had been nothing but a violent rush of emotion which had nothing to do with their real lives. Even now nothing had really changed. Their brief time together was spent in a vacuum.

He saw the clouds which had shadowed her eyes, but he did not enquire what had caused them. He had a pretty good idea, and some things were best left unspoken. Why go out and find hurt when it waited like a shadowy figure just around the corner? Instead, he touched her cheek. 'And when did *you* last have a holiday?'

'Last year. I went to Australia to visit an old schoolfriend. She's settled down there—married an Aussie.' The spark of an idea began to form in her mind. 'Wouldn't it be lovely to have a break together, Hashim?' She looked around at the lavish yet soulless bedroom. 'Somewhere that wasn't in a hotel?'

He played along with her fantasy as she had played along with so many of his. 'And where would we go?'

Sienna put her head to one side and considered. 'I guess we'd stay in England. Travelling abroad would be too much hassle, and you travel too much anyway.

It would be somewhere you could be completely incognito—completely free.'

'Does such a place exist?' he mocked.

Sienna nodded. 'I know of a beautiful old converted farmhouse—it's right in the middle of nowhere. I hired it once for a rock star's fortieth birthday and everyone was raving on about it.'

'But where would my bodyguards stay?'

'There's a cottage in the grounds. Not too far and yet far enough...'

Her voice tailed off and he read the erotic promise in her eyes. An unbearable temptation crept over him. Something was going to have to give in his life soon, and he knew that it was going to be his relationship with Sienna. But before it did...

Couldn't he have the briefest taste of what it was like to be 'normal'? Just an ordinary man taking a holiday with a woman who excited and calmed and provoked and stimulated him in dizzying succession? Someone who was part of his past and now his present, but could never be part of his future...

'Can you arrange it?' he questioned suddenly.

Sienna blinked. 'You're serious?'

'Yes.' He did a quick calculation in his head. 'I can manage next weekend, if that fits in with your job?'

She was too excited to notice the faint sarcasm in his voice. Or to question whether two weekends on the trot was not pushing their luck.

She nodded. 'Well, yes—of course I can. If we can

get it. It's quite short notice—but it should be fine. I mean—who in their right mind wants to holiday in the English countryside in the middle of February?'

'Well, I do.'

They looked at one another and Sienna started giggling.

'So do I.'

CHAPTER ELEVEN

THERE was a huge fireplace, an ancient-looking kitchen, and a bed in the main upstairs room which looked exactly as it must have done a century before.

The bodyguards were settled in the cottage by the main gate, with a widescreen TV and the promise of a huge, no-questions-asked bonus, and Sienna and Hashim were finally on their own.

'It is like stepping back in time,' Hashim murmured, his black eyes fascinated as he glanced around him. 'And it's freezing.'

'Yes, it is.' She turned to him. 'Can you light a fire?'

His smile touched on the arrogant. 'Naturally.'

'Well, then—over to you. I'm going to make us something to eat.'

But he shook his head. If they were playing honeymoon—which he rather imagined that they were—then there was something far more pressing than food or fuel on the agenda. 'You want to eat food?' he murmured. 'Or to eat me?'

'You are outrageous!' she protested, but only half-heartedly, for his hands had slithered underneath her sweater and were making her nipples grow very hard indeed. 'We...we ought to draw the curtains,' she said breathlessly.

She went and yanked across the faded chintz and he came up behind her, skimming his hands down over her hips. 'Mmm. I am pleased to see that you are wearing a skirt.'

'Because my Sheikh does not like jeans,' she said demurely, and closed her eyes as she felt him reach beneath it to graze his fingers over her searing heat.

'You are ready,' he observed, on a slight note of surprise.

'I've been ready for hours,' she admitted, hopping and almost stumbling in her eagerness to help him take off her panties.

'So have I,' he admitted huskily.

They only made it as far as the big, old-fashioned sprung sofa, where Hashim kicked off his trousers and then pulled her down onto his lap, guiding her slowly over his aching shaft before plunging deep inside her.

'Oh!' she moaned, as he filled her completely, moving her up and down until she thought that she could bear it no longer. Almost before she could believe it to be happening she felt herself begin to dissolve.

And Hashim felt it, too—shatteringly and simultaneously—and as her body began to convulse out its pleasure so did his follow, in almost complete harmony. And in those few last seconds before the power of it temporarily obliterated consciousness their eyes met, locked and held.

'Sienna!' he gasped as she began to shudder around him, and her name seemed to be torn from his soul.

'Hashim!' she breathed brokenly, her fingers digging into the rich silk of his skin. *If only I could tell you how much I love you.*

For a while they stayed just like that, Sienna still astride him, gazing down and stroking her hand along the rugged outline of his jaw.

'What are you thinking?' he questioned softly.

That what should never have happened had done so. That the falling in love was complete. That it was too late to stop herself and protect herself. And it had happened just at the time when she suspected it was all coming to an end.

'You should never ask a woman something like that after making love to her.'

Not when she's vulnerable enough to tell you something you won't want to hear. She shivered a little as the flush of passion on her skin began to fade.

'Better get that fire going,' she said lightly, and climbed off him.

Escaping into the kitchen while he built the fire, she made soup from organic vegetables and served it with chunky wholemeal bread, and cheese which had come straight from the nearby farm. They quenched their thirst with elderflower water and then drank scented tea, sitting on a furry rug in front of the gradually roaring fire.

'Do you like that?' she asked.

'Perfect,' he said, but there was a sudden heaviness in his heart.

They watched a video of Sienna's favourite film—an old musical which soon had her sniffing like a hay-fever sufferer.

'You're crying!' he accused.

'No, I'm not—it's just a corny old film,' she said crossly.

'Come here,' he said.

And, even though it made her heart ache, she went.

They spent their time doing simple things. Wrapping up warm before walking over the crunchy morning frost which hardly had time to melt before a setting crimson sun turned the fields into fire every afternoon.

His bodyguards seemed quite content to be doing their own thing, and there wasn't a peep out of his phone. Once they even ventured into the small local pub for lunch, and if anyone wondered why there was a big, dark car sitting gleaming in the car park, no-body bothered asking.

The real world seemed such a long way away, and part of Sienna fervently wished it could stay that way. If it weren't for his position they could live a life like this all the time. He was right—she *had* always taken her freedom for granted—and never had she cherished it more than during this weekend.

She watched him relax. Saw the dark shadows melt away from beneath his eyes and the tiny, fan-like creases at the corners of his black eyes ironed out as if by magic.

And for Hashim it was a provocative glimpse of a life he could never really know. He had not felt as unencumbered as this since those long-ago days of falconing in the mountains of Qudamah.

'Ah, Sienna,' he said on their last morning, when they sat eating pancakes for breakfast. 'Don't you wish that life could always be this simple?'

She smiled, knowing full well that there was no point in coming out with a stock phrase like: It *could* be like this. Because it couldn't.

She put the lid back on the golden syrup. 'Do you want to listen to the radio?'

Hashim frowned. 'What for?'

'Well, Qudamah seems to have been in the news a lot lately.'

Funny how you could look for an opportunity to say something and then find, when it came, that you wished you didn't have to. He gazed down at the clear amber of the delicate tea. 'There is going to be an election very soon—and elections always demand a lot of my time.' He looked at her. 'I am going to have to fly back tomorrow.'

Sienna nodded. 'I know you are.'

He drew in a deep breath. 'And I'm not sure when I'll be back.'

She felt the tendril of long-held fear finally wrapping itself around her heart. 'I know that, too.' Don't make him have to say it. Accept what is inevitable.

Make it easy on yourself. 'Hashim, it's okay. You don't have to say it. I know it's over.'

He didn't deny it, but the dark eyes which he lifted to her face were troubled. 'I do not wish this, Sienna—but increasingly I recognise that my place is in my homeland, not here.' He gave a restless little movement of his shoulders. 'There are obligations I now need to fulfil. And I don't want to tie you down to a relationship which can never go anywhere. Or to make you a promise I am unable to keep. If this fades into failed intentions and meetings which never happen then all that we will have left to remember is bitterness.' His voice grew hard. 'And I cannot face that. Not for a second time. Not when…'

The words were there in his mouth, just begging to be said. But words could be dishonest—even if you meant them. They could open up all kinds of unrealistic expectations. If he tried to explain how much she had come to mean to him then would that not tie her to him anyway—no matter how much he tried not to let it? What if she started seeing them as star-crossed lovers instead of just getting on with her life?

She saw the discomfiture on his face and jumped in to rescue the situation—or rather to rescue herself. She had had more with him than any woman could have hoped to have, and she would ensure that he remembered her with dignity.

'It's been wonderful. Gorgeous. It was a fine affair,' she said softly. 'But now it's over.'

His eyes narrowed. He had expected…what? That

she might at least shed a tear for him! Or that her face might indicate some feelings of dejection! His pride was hurt, yet his pain came from deeper feelings than pride. He pushed them away with an instinct borne out of self-protection. 'You seem almost pleased about it,' he observed coolly.

'Oh, Hashim,' she said impatiently. 'Of course I'm not *pleased* about it—but I recognise that it has to be, so what's the alternative?'

Women had begged him before—many times. They had shed tears and clung to him. Hadn't there been a selfish side which had thought that Sienna might do the same? For if she behaved like all the others, then wouldn't that make it easier for him to walk away from her without another thought?

But there had never been another relationship like this one, he recognised. Nor ever would be again. His destiny would not allow it—for his flings and his freedom must now be curtailed. The luxurious but weighty doors of his royal prison were waiting to clang shut on him, and if he took himself down the path of useless and indulgent analysis then what good would it do him? Or her?

'Come here,' he said simply, and opened his arms.

Sienna didn't need to be told that this was the last time. It was written in his eyes and spoken in every lingering kiss and caress. His hands and his fingers seemed as though they were discovering her for the first time, and yet bidding her farewell as they did so.

'Oh, Hashim,' she said, in a choked kind of voice.

'Let us lie once more in that old bed,' he whispered, and she nodded.

He carried her up the rickety staircase towards the room they had shared, bending his head so as not to knock it on one of the dark beams, and put her down as carefully as if she had been a cherished and delicate piece of filagree.

Their undressing was slow and silent, and as she sank back into feather pillows his dark body moved over hers. She thought about how many couples had lain in this bed, like this. How many children had been conceived—maybe even born here? Ghostly generations of long-ago lovers joined them—wordlessly entering the indefinable space between past and present. For at what point did the present become the past?

Their climax would bring an end to it all, and the sex would become just a memory. As would the rest. She trembled as Hashim thrust into her with a hunger and a poignancy which made hot salt tears slide from beneath her eyelids.

'Ah, Sienna. Don't cry,' he said afterwards, wiping the tracks away with his finger.

They lay there for a while without sleeping, and then Sienna stirred. Be the first to make a move, she told herself. Don't put yourself in the position of being the deserted one.

'I'd better go and pack up the kitchen.'

He tightened his hold on her waist. 'I can have one of the guards come over and do it.'

But she shook her head and prised his fingers away as if she was removing a clam from the side of a rock. 'No, Hashim—that will defeat the object of our ordinary weekend. I'll go and chuck all the leftover food away—you can wash the dishes.'

He was torn between outrage and humour. 'Yes, Sienna,' he murmured, but his heart was heavy.

They were quiet in the car on the drive back, even though the driver was firmly locked away behind soundproof glass. It had begun to rain, and through the tinted windows she could see droplets battering against the glass, as if the heavens themselves were sobbing.

It was only when they were approaching South Kensington that he laid one dark hand on hers.

'You will come back to the hotel with me?'

'No.'

He asked for no explanation; but then he had known what her answer would be. 'Sienna?'

She turned her head back to face him and her green eyes were sombre, but there was a soft dignity about her which took his breath away. He thought about how often in the past he had been able to persuade her to do something against her will just by the sheer power of the sexual chemistry which existed between them, but he recognised now that nothing he could do would change her mind. Not this time.

Something had changed. In her. In him. In them both. For not only would she refuse to succumb to him, he would no longer make an attempt to have her bend to his will. Somewhere along the way they had become equals, and for Hashim it was a bittersweet awakening. An awareness that it had come at the wrong time—but could it have ever been the right time?

Not with Sienna, no.

He bent down to the Qudamah-crested dispatch box which accompanied him everywhere and pulled out a slim leather box. He held it out towards her but she shook her head, the thick dark hair flying like a storm.

'No, Hashim!' She would not be paid off—have him bid her farewell with the expensive baubles she had previously refused to accept. 'Whatever it is, I don't want it. I don't want your diamonds or your emeralds, thank you very much! I told you a long time ago that I could not and would not be bought, and I meant it!'

He laughed softly. 'I know you did, my fiery Sienna,' he murmured. 'And I think that your expectations of costly gems are a little wide of the mark.' He put the box in her hand and closed her fingers around it, his black eyes washing over her. 'Please. Open it.'

Something in his manner made her obey him, her fingers trembling as she flicked open the catch to see a necklace lying against indigo velvet. But it was no ordinary necklace. The chain was as fine as a sliver of light and in the centre of it lay a tiny golden bird.

'H-Hashim?' she questioned shakily.

'Here.' He lifted it from the box and placed it into

the centre of her palm, where the fine chain lay coiled like an elegant snake, the small charm gleaming like the sun.

'What is it?'

'It is an eagle—a golden eagle. She flies on the flag of Qudamah and is the symbol of my country—for she represents freedom and power. This is the only time you will ever see her chained.'

Like him. The thought flew unbidden into her mind. Freedom and power and never to be chained. She studied it intently, focusing fiercely on the workmanship because at least that kept the tears at bay. 'It's...beautiful.'

'Shall I put it on for you?'

Sienna nodded, unable to speak for fear that she would blurt out words which could never be taken back. Words of love which would mortify him and make their parting even more painful.

He slid his hands around her neck, wanting so much to linger there—to raise the heavy weight of her hair so that he could kiss the soft nape and then turn her head to take her lips, coaxing their luscious warmth into eager response.

'I thought you were going to put it on?'

Her faintly bemused voice disrupted his troubled thoughts. 'So I was.' He clipped it in place. 'There.'

For a moment their eyes met, and the pain which smote at her heart made her feel dizzy and weak. Turning her head to look out of the window with the desperation of a drowning woman struggling towards the surface for light and air, Sienna saw with relief that they were at the end of her road.

'Well, here we are! Thank you, Hashim.' She leaned forward. The touch of her mouth against his was fleeting and the pain increased. 'Take very good care.'

He touched her fingertips to his lips and as she pushed open the car door said something in his native tongue to the driver, who got out and removed her one small bag from the boot.

The tinted window slid silently down and all she could see were glittering black eyes—the only thing which seemed truly alive in the tight mask of his face. She flashed him a smile, and then she turned away.

Somehow she made it inside without crying, but once there the tears began to pour down her cheeks without stopping. Kat was away and she was glad, because it gave her time to get over the worst, to recover on her own like a wounded animal.

There was no one to tell her to eat. No one to question why she couldn't sleep. No one to tell her that it was wrong to shed her tears and that there were plenty more fish in the sea. Maybe there were—but none like Hashim.

By the third day she had begun to feel a little better. Her heart was aching, but she knew that Hashim would hate it if she became one of those women who let their whole lives collapse around them because a love affair hadn't worked out.

She bathed and washed her hair, and was just pulling on a big black sweater which virtually came down to her knees when the doorbell rang. She wondered if it was Kat back, having forgotten her keys.

She opened the door, completely unprepared to see the batallion of photographers who were jostling for position, jerking back in alarm as the multiple flash from their array of cameras temporarily blinded her. Someone thrust a phallic-looking microphone under her chin.

'Miss Baker!' called a TV-trained voice. 'Sienna! Is the Sheikh of Qudamah aware that you used to be a topless model?'

CHAPTER TWELVE

THE startled doorstep photo made the first edition and the second—only it ran alongside a much larger photo. There was her sand-sprinkled and sultry image plastered over all the tabloids.

Even the serious broadsheets gave it house-room—justifying their usual no-breasts policy with weighty pieces on the changing morals of the Middle East. And a censored version of it was beamed into homes the length and breadth of the country as an add-on to an otherwise boring television news show.

'And finally, the Sheikh of the fiercely traditional State of Qudamah is rumoured to be dating a British glamour model. Stunning brunette Sienna Baker…'

Female leader-writers took up the case in their mid-week columns, asking righteously: *What would you do if your son brought a topless model home?*

Trapped inside the house, unable to go out without fear of being accosted, Sienna was sitting in the kitchen at the back of the house with the blinds drawn down when Kat came in and handed her the telephone with a look which said everything.

She pressed the phone to her ear. She wasn't aware she'd actually said anything, but she must have made some sort of sound because she heard his deep and silky voice.

'Sienna?'

She bit her lip. Closed her eyes. She wouldn't cry. She *wouldn't*. But the sound of his dear voice was almost more than she could bear. 'Yes, it's me.'

'Are you all right?'

'Ask me another. How about you?'

He ignored that. 'The press are still there?'

'Well, not so many of them. I think they got fed up because I refused to say anything.'

'Good. If you feed a story it only grows.'

'Oh, Hashim—how the hell did they get hold of it? How did they even find out about it?'

Hashim's mouth tightened into a grim and forbidding line. He suspected that someone in Qudamah must have informed the foreign press about a juicy piece of gossip in their Ruler's life. In the power-play that was his life Sienna's past had become a weapon. And he must protect her from the fall-out.

'These things have a habit of getting out,' he said slowly. 'That's the way the world works.'

He sounded almost weary, as if he had seen sides of the world she did not know—and of course he had. She couldn't imagine what it must be like to be a sheikh, but she was fairly sure that it would be very hard to trust people's motives towards you. 'Yes,' said quietly. 'I imagine so.'

The silence between them seemed huge. 'I am sending some people to look after you, Sienna. If I come myself it will only add fire to the story. Is there somewhere you can go?'

She was suddenly and acutely aware that this conversation was a purely practical one, and not personal at all. He didn't want to talk—not *really* talk—and besides, what was there left to say? This was damage limitation time.

She bit her lip. Where did she always turn when she wanted an escape route? Who would always accept her with open arms and no questions asked? Who wanted the best for her no matter what. 'My mother wants me to go to her.'

'Then go. Let me arrange it.'

'Hashim—you don't seem to understand!' she said frustratedly. 'I have existing contracts to fulfil. And the phone hasn't stopped ringing with work requests—I've never been so popular. I think it's the curiosity factor,' she added acidly. 'Having your party planned by a so-called ''Glamour Model.'' But some of the calls are from journalists pretending to be clients. I'm certain of it.'

He felt the dark dagger of self-contempt as he remembered that he too had done just that. Pretended. Masqueraded. Finally got his way by seducing her— and now what had happened? Had she ever deserved this because of some rash youthful decision made with all the best intentions? 'I'm sorry,' he said quietly.

She shook her head as if he was in the room, hating to hear his apology—so stilted and formal—like one stranger talking to another. 'It isn't your fault, it's mine. I should never have done it in the first place—I just didn't realise it was going to come back and haunt me in such a big way.'

'But that is down to me. To your relationship with me.'

The most precious thing in her life. *Past tense*, she reminded herself. She sighed, wanting to lean on him yet knowing she shouldn't. And anyway, she couldn't—not really. He was at his Palace, thousands of miles away, and she was holed up in her tiny terraced house in Kennington. There were no arms to hold her, no heart to beat next to hers, no hand to stroke her hair.

'Can you get someone else to honour your existing contracts and ignore all the others?' he demanded.

'And who is going to pay my mortgage in the meantime?'

There was a moment's silence, and Hashim chose his words with fastidious care, knowing that he trod on very sensitive ground here. 'That is simple. You must let me help you, Sienna.'

She froze. 'What do you mean—*help* me?'

He could hear the bristly defensiveness which spiked her voice and, while he silently applauded her fierce pride, he knew that it would not and could not serve her well—not in circumstances such as these. 'Just hear me out without interruption. That is all I ask of you. Please, Sienna, it is vital,' he said softly.

'If I took care of your mortgage for you—would that not free you up to get away for a while?'

'I'm not letting you pay for me!' Her voice lowered. 'You must be able to see why I stand so firm on this issue.'

For a moment he had to control the instinctive lash of his tongue. Stubborn woman! Could she not see that he was only trying to help her?

Drawing on diplomatic reserves he had never had to call on before, he tried again. 'Sienna,' he said patiently. 'I admire your independence and your spirit, but this is not some showering of expensive baubles on a mistress—this is me trying to help you get out of a bad situation which is mostly of my doing. To make some kind of amends. Will you not let me do that for you? Would not all that has grown between us be completely worthless if you will not allow me to behave as any true friend would towards another?'

There was silence. How appalled he would be if he knew that her thoughts were not of indignation that he was trying to buy her out of something but instead had fixed upon a word which resonated cruelly round and round in her head. Who would ever have thought that the acknowledgement that he was her *friend* could have unwittingly caused so much heartache?

'Will you let me?' he said.

What choice did she have? To brazen it out in London, aware of the eyes which followed her? The curious glances? Women looking down their noses at her and men looking…? Well, she didn't even want to go *there*.

'In a few weeks all the fuss will have died down,' he continued smoothly. 'The news will have moved on. That's what happens.'

And, stupidly, that upset her even more—for once it had died down it really would be over. And wasn't there a part of her—ever while loathing all this fuss and attention—that was secretly glad because it had brought Hashim back into her life when she'd thought that he had gone for good?

'All right. I'll go to my mother's,' she said.

At the other end of the phone, Hashim closed his eyes with relief. Outside his private study the court was in uproar, and Abdul-Aziz was prowling round the palace like a starving tom-cat, but Hashim didn't care. She was safe. She would be safe—he had the resources to protect her.

'I will have a car sent immediately,' he said, glad now that he could rely on action, for this was something he always felt comfortable with. 'And bodyguards will be placed at the entrance to your mother's home.'

She opened her mouth to say that he didn't even know where her mother lived, but then shut it again. Of course he did. He knew everything—and if he didn't he could get someone to find out for him. Hashim could get anything he pleased.

'Thank you, Hashim,' she said.

'Don't thank me,' he said fiercely. 'Just stay strong.

Can you do that?' He nearly said *for me*—except that in the circumstances he knew he had no right to ask.

She allowed herself to picture him, and knew she would not crumble. 'As an ox,' she said huskily.

Hashim closed his eyes. 'Or an eagle,' he whispered.

'Goodbye,' she whispered back, and put the phone down before she began to cry. Because although the structure of her life had been torn apart it didn't even register on the pain-scale.

Nothing touched her and nothing could—other than the heartbreak of not being with the man she loved.

CHAPTER THIRTEEN

'DARLING, calm down, sit down, and drink that cup of tea before it gets cold!'

Sienna sniffed and smiled, and took a sip of the fragrant Earl Grey. How some things never changed!

'That's better,' said her mother approvingly, brushing some mud from the leg of her jodhpurs and dunking a digestive biscuit into her own tea.

'Mum, I'm so sorry—'

'Oh, fiddlesticks!' said her mother cheerfully. 'It's done my reputation no end of good locally—I'll never be asked to judge the prize cauliflower section at the village show again!' She sighed. 'I was getting rather bored with it, if the truth were known.'

'No, I'm serious.'

'And so am I, Sienna,' said her mother firmly. 'In my opinion you look rather lovely in those photos— and if you compare them to some of the nudes in our national galleries, why, they're positively tame! It's all a question of perception. I admit that when you first did it I was angry—but not for long. How could I be when the money you earned from it meant that I could have my operation? I thanked you then from the bottom of my heart and I still do.' She finished her biscuit and edged her fingers towards another.

'Better not. Now, what I really want to know is— what's this young sheikh of yours really like?'

This, in a way, was even harder than explaining that for the time being there were two hefty bodyguards stationed at the front gate.

'He's not young, Mum,' said Sienna. 'He's thirty-five.'

'Oh, positively ancient!'

'And he isn't…' No, this, *this* was the hardest part. 'He isn't mine. Not any more. He never was, really.' She put her cup down and stared candidly at her mother. 'I just had a relationship with him,' she said defiantly.

'Well, thank heavens for that!' murmured her mother. 'I was beginning to wonder when you'd find yourself a boyfriend.'

'Mum!'

'Well, you never seemed really interested.'

There was a question in her mother's eyes, and for the first time in her life Sienna spoke to her not as a mother but as another woman. 'I went out with Hashim years ago—a couple of years after I did the photos, actually,' she said quietly. 'And he was a pretty hard act to follow.'

Her mother replied in kind. 'I'm not surprised,' she said softly. 'He looks absolutely gorgeous.'

'Well, he is—but he just happens to be a sheikh and there's no future in it. He comes from a fiercely traditional country and anyway—he doesn't love me.'

'Are you sure he doesn't?'

'Of course I'm sure!'

'He didn't have to go to all the trouble of arranging protection for you, did he? Or deliver that gorgeous hamper and massive bouquet of flowers for me.' She stared happily at the massed display of blooms which were currently making the sitting room look like a florist's shop.

How could her mother ever begin to understand that for a man of Hashim's untold wealth such gestures were mere drops in a limitless ocean? 'He feels guilty,' she said flatly. 'This would never have erupted if it hadn't been for his position. That's all.'

'Have it your own way, darling—if you want to be stubborn, then I can't stop you. Now.' Her mother beamed at her. 'Do you want to see if you can fit into your old jodhpurs and give me a hand in the stables? A bit of good old-fashioned fresh air and exercise is just what the doctor ordered. Then later I've asked Kirsty over for tea. Cara is *three* now. Can you believe it?' She smiled. 'It only seems a minute ago since you and Kirsty were toddling off to nursery together at the same age.'

Sienna smiled too, because the thought of seeing her old friend was strangely comforting. It was all too easy to let friendships slip—though time and distance played their part. Sometimes she wondered what would have happened if she'd taken Kirsty's path in life—stayed around and married a local farmer, then started producing a brood of children. Would that have guaranteed her personal happiness?

It wasn't that easy, she decided, as she struggled into her old riding clothes. It wasn't the place you chose or the job you ended up doing—it was all to do with the man you ended up falling in love with and the path that took you on.

And she had just had the misfortune to fall for someone who wasn't taking her anywhere.

But her mother was right—the fresh air and exercise *did* work their own kind of magic. Physically, at least. The aching in her heart needed the kind of remedy which never provided instant healing. It needed time.

She got up at first light and went down to the stables. She did all the mucky stuff and some of the fun stuff too—for there was nothing more rewarding than watching fearful children grow in confidence as they began to master the skill of riding. Life suddenly seemed very simple—and her busy London existence like something which had happened in a past life.

She had thought she would miss the networking and the hectic pace of making people's party dreams come true, but she didn't. She just wished that she had the power to fulfil her own personal dreams, but she didn't. Besides, you shouldn't rely on a man to make you happy, she told herself. Everyone knew that.

And Cara was a delight—homing in on Sienna straight away, her eyes wide when it was explained that Mummy and Sienna had been just the same age as her once upon a time!

She had a habit of sticking her little tongue out of the corner of her mouth when she was thinking.

'Can I play with Sienna, Mummy?' she asked one day.

Kirsty shot her a glance. 'Oh, Sienna's far too busy—'

'No,' said Sienna firmly. 'No, I'm not, and I want Cara to come and play. We could make cupcakes one day if you like?'

'With chocolate chips?'

'Yes, darling—I *love* chocolate chips—and we can use those little silver balls too, if you're very good.'

At least there was plenty to keep her occupied—leaving little time for wafting around the house missing her lover. But probably the hardest part of all was accepting that it really *was* over. Because in a way things seemed just the same. Their feelings hadn't changed and they normally had weeks in between seeing one another anyway.

If only they could have rowed—or stopped speaking entirely—then she might have found it easier to believe that it was over. Easier? Well, maybe not. That was asking too much. What's it going to take to forget him? she asked herself. An announcement that he's going to marry someone else, as one day you know he will?

Sienna was making more cakes with Cara one afternoon when her mother came rushing into the kitchen.

'One of the bodyguards has just knocked!' she babbled excitedly. 'There is a visitor on the way to see you!'

Sienna's heart missed a beat. She held the wooden spoon in the air as if it was a magic wand—and, oh, how she wished it was. She would wave it, and...

'Is it Hashim?' she breathed.

'Oh, darling, no—I'm afraid it isn't. It's a man called...' Her mother frowned as she concentrated on saying his name correctly. 'Abdul-Aziz.'

Sienna hoped her face did not betray her disappointment. 'Then you'd better show him in,' she said courteously.

Abdul-Aziz swept into her mother's low-beamed kitchen as if he owned the place. It had been a long time since Sienna had seen him, and in his way he was no less formidable—his eyes still looked like raisins which had been created in the Arctic and his mouth was set in such a way as to show he meant business.

But some of the hardness of his features had dissolved, and Sienna found herself wondering if that was down to the calming effects of married life. Or was she in danger of attributing her own wistfulness to other people?

Five years ago she had been utterly intimidated by him, but a lot had changed since then. For a start she had grown up—but, more importantly, she had shared something very special with Hashim. He had given her confidence and belief in herself as a woman—and nothing could take that away from her.

Abdul-Aziz's eyes narrowed as he saw her, and Sienna was aware that she could not have looked worse—old clothes, no make-up, covered in cake mix, with a tiny girl clinging onto her apron and demanding to know, 'Who's that cross man?'

'It's someone I know,' she whispered, and looked at her mother. 'Would you mind finishing the cakes with Cara while I take my visitor into the sitting room?'

Cara snuffled a bit, and her mother looked disappointed that she wasn't going to get a ringside seat to hear whatever the 'cross man' had to say, but Sienna felt strangely serene as she led Abdul-Aziz across the hall and into the chintzy room. The worst had already happened and Hashim was not with her. Nothing could touch her now.

She looked across the room at him, and she'd have been lying if she hadn't admitted deriving a little pleasure from the look of perplexity on Abdul-Aziz's face. Had he been expecting her to be lolling around in some over-the-top boudoir, wearing nothing but a pair of racy stockings and suspenders?

'Would you like tea, Mr Aziz?' she asked politely. 'I'm not quite sure how to address you.'

'You can call me Abdul,' he said grudgingly. 'And, no, I don't want tea. Thank you,' he added, as if he had just remembered something.

Like his manners, thought Sienna wryly—for he gave the distinct impression of a man who was struggling to contain himself.

'What can I do for you?' she murmured.

'That child.' He cocked his head in the direction of the door. 'She is your child?'

Sienna started to say of course not—but there was no 'of course' about it—not in his eyes. If she suddenly produced a spellbook and started chanting incantations she didn't think he'd bat an eyelid.

'No,' she answered quietly. 'She is the child of my schoolfriend.'

Now he was staring at the tiny golden eagle which dangled around her slender neck and which she never took off.

'And my Sheikh gave you this?' he demanded.

'I suspect you already know the answer to that one. Yes. He did.'

He tossed his head back like a stallion about to rear up. 'You must renounce him!' he declared dramatically. 'Unequivocally and immediately!'

Sienna stared at him. 'I beg your pardon?'

'You have not heard?' he demanded.

'I haven't got a clue what you're talking about.'

'He has not told you?'

This hurt. 'No.'

'Sheikh Hashim is planning to go on State television and make an announcement!'

'What kind of announcement?'

Abdul-Aziz's mouth tightened. 'He refuses to say…stubborn boy!…but I know in my heart what it will be.'

'You do? You're some kind of mind-reader, are you?'

'He is going to declare his love for you!' he hissed.

Sienna's laugh was genuine, but it was tinged with sadness. 'You'd never make money out of clairvoyancy, Abdul,' she said. 'It's over between me and Hashim—he's not in love with me.'

'He isn't?' His suspicious look cleared and was replaced by an expression of bright hope. 'You are certain of this?'

'Yes.'

'Then what is he plotting?' questioned Abdul-Aziz to himself thoughtfully.

'Don't you think you should come right out and ask him yourself?'

'I have. He would tell me nothing.'

'Then it's very *disloyal* of you to come sneaking over here behind his back, trying to find out things he obviously doesn't wish to tell you.'

He glared at her. 'While your loyalty to the Sheikh is admirable, I am not used to being spoken to in such a way, Miss Baker. Especially by a woman.'

'How come I'm not surprised?' Sienna murmured.

'Will you try to stop him?' he persisted.

'I wouldn't dream of it,' said Sienna calmly. 'And even if I wanted to, I couldn't. He is a man in charge of his own destiny.' She stared at him. 'As we all are.'

An odd, calculating light came into Abdul-Aziz's

strange, cold eyes. 'Yes, indeed we are,' he said. 'You are a strong woman, Miss Baker.'

Was she? At that moment she felt a mixture of strength and weakness, but her strength came from her unwavering love for Hashim. And so too, in a way, did her weakness. 'Thank you, Abdul.'

The cold eyes narrowed. Had they softened fractionally, or had she just imagined it? 'You have a message for him?'

Tell him I love him. Tell him I can't stop thinking about him. Tell him that if I really did have magical powers then I would use them all to protect and guard him from evil for the rest of his life.

'Just tell him Sienna says hello.'

'Hello?' he echoed faintly, and then nodded, giving a deep bow before leaving the room.

Sienna felt as if she was operating on some kind of autopilot as she continued with the ritual of decorating cupcakes with Cara. She realised that she was waiting for something, but was not quite sure how she knew—or what, indeed, she was waiting for.

But then her mobile phone rang, and she knew who it would be even before she saw 'Hashim' flashing on the screen. Her heart started beating fit to burst.

'Sienna?'

'Abdul has been to see me,' she blurted out.

'I know he has.'

'You didn't think to warn me?'

'Did you need me to?' he questioned coolly.

'He says you're going to broadcast to the nation.'

emptied he stood staring at her for long, countless seconds.

'Now come to me,' he commanded.

She went like a woman willingly sleepwalking. Towards him. Summoned by her Sheikh. Into his arms. The place where she most wanted to be.

There was no kiss, just a fierce embrace which seemed to force all the breath out of her lungs. He clasped her against him and pressed his face to her scented hair. His words were muffled.

'You know that I love you, don't you, Sienna?'

Sienna pulled away and stared up at him, her eyes blinking rapidly, certain that she must have misheard him. 'Hashim?'

'Can't you feel it in the beating of my heart?' He placed her palm over his chest, where the rapid thundering of his life-blood made her eyes widen in dawning realisation. 'It is no good, Sienna—for I have tried. By the mountains and the rivers, I have tried! I have attempted the impossible and have failed. To forget you. To imagine life without you. And I cannot. *I will not.*'

'But *love*?' she whispered.

'Yes, love.' He smiled. 'More powerful than the eagle—a force as powerful as life itself—can you not feel it gathering strength, Sienna—as the bird itself does just before flight?'

He waited.

But Sienna felt tongue-tied and strangely humble—and scared too, in these imposing surroundings. A declaration she had longed for and never thought to hear—and now that it had been made she was shaken. It was as if dust had turned to gold before her eyes, and she was terrified that it would change back to dust again.

Yet he was right. She could feel the strength emanating from him—waves of it washing over her barely believing self. She touched her fingertips to the charm at her neck, as if it could give her the courage to say the words to him. Words she had once had tossed back in her face. Words she had grown inside her for so long, all the while trying to deny them.

'I love you too,' Hashim,' she said brokenly. 'I have done right from the very start, and it never changed—never dimmed—even when I prayed that it would.' She stared into the black eyes which had softened now. 'But you knew that, didn't you? You could read it in my eyes.'

'Yes.'

'And it doesn't actually *change* anything, does it? Not practically. You're still a sheikh and I'm still a—'

'No!' He cut her words off with brutal force. 'Do not say it! You are more and then much more—but you are not that! A youthful folly does not define a person for the rest of their lives!'

'But that is how I will be perceived.'

'And that,' he said grimly, '*that* is why I am making the broadcast. They are setting up cameras in the small Throne Room.' He tilted his head—handsome and irresistible. 'Will you come in with me?'

'What are you going to say?'

'Will you come in with me?' he repeated inexorably.

'Yes.'

'And I must ask you something else, Sienna—and this is important. The life you live in England is incompatible with mine. My home is here. My place is here—increasingly more so. Could you renounce much of the freedom you enjoy in England? Is your love for me strong enough to embrace my life here? For if you decide to, you must do so without reservation. There can be no trial period, no waiting to see whether or not you can adapt. It must be a leap of faith and nothing less. You must decide whether your love for me is strong enough to commit to me, and to commit for the rest of your life. When you marry me,' he finished deliberately, his gaze fixed firmly on her face.

'*Marry* you?' she echoed, genuinely shocked.

Wry amusement vied with outrage in his black eyes. 'You think that I would contemplate any alternative to marriage?' he demanded. 'That I should not want you as my wife? Assuming,' he added arrogantly, 'that you wish to be my wife? But if you do then you will be taking on more than most women do, and you must be certain in your heart that your destiny is beside me.'

Sienna licked her lips. She thought of the eagle which hung around her neck—powerful and fearless—the symbol of his country. This strange land with a tongue that was foreign to her. A place so very different from all that she had known—and yet it contained the only thing which was important to her.

Hashim.

Was she fearless enough in her love to grasp it tightly and never let it go? To make her vows to him and mean them? Never to leave his side? To promise to be true, no matter what life threw in their path? But wasn't that what *all* marriages were supposed to mean?

'Oh, yes,' she whispered. 'Yes, yes, and a million times yes.' There was an odd kind of lump in her throat. 'But will your people accept me?'

'If they want me as their Ruler, then they will have to.'

'Do you want to take that chance?'

'I can't not,' he said simply. But he knew that he could never rule—nor would be fit to rule—if he allowed his people to prevent him from seizing his heart's desire. Because any man who turned away from one of life's greatest mysteries could never be a complete man.

'But...' Sienna bit her lip, not wanting to destroy the beautiful magic his words of love had created, but knowing that she must not hide behind her fears, must face them head-on—even if expressing them might put paid to all her future happiness.

'But what, my beautiful Sienna?' he prompted softly as he saw the hurt and the pain in her eyes.

'The photos.' It came out in a bitter sigh. 'What if

your people see that calendar—how on earth would they ever accept me then?'

'They shall not see it,' he breathed. 'Not now and not ever.'

He sounded so certain that she stared up at him in bewilderment. 'How can you be so sure?'

'Because I have bought up all the rights to those photos—they are now exclusively mine. No newspaper will ever publish them, the calendar shall never be reprinted, and the negatives have been destroyed. I have even made sure that they will never appear on the infernal internet,' he finished grimly.

She opened her mouth to ask how, but then changed her mind. When you were as rich and as powerful and as determined as Hashim, then Sienna supposed anything was possible. Instead, she gave a rather wobbly smile, needing something more than words or reassurance now. Something which she had missed so unbearably. She was aching to have him touch her again. 'Won't you please kiss me?' she whispered.

He felt a strange kick to his heart as he bent his face to hers. Was it a kind of weakness for a man to be so in thrall to one woman? 'You wish your Sheikh to go before the cameras in a state of arousal?' he murmured.

'Oh, Hashim—I never thought of that! I've got so much to learn. Maybe we'd better not…'

He gave a low, rumbling laugh. 'And you think that I have not been aroused since the moment you first walked in, my love? That I can look at you without wanting you? Then, yes, you still have much to learn! Now, come here.'

It was a brief kiss, fuelled by a sense of coming home rather than passion—though that was bubbling away beneath the surface as his lips brushed over hers.

'Now,' he said firmly, and, bending down, rang a small golden bell.

A stream of people began to appear. Men in flowing robes who bowed briefly to her and then deeper still to Hashim. And then they were walking along cool marble corridors towards the 'small' Throne Room—which seemed pretty vast to Sienna, but there again she hadn't had much experience of them.

She had been in TV studios before, but never when everyone had been behaving with such genuine deference towards the interviewee.

Hashim settled her in a chair at the back of the room and she watched while the camera lights lit up his face like the brightest sunshine. And then the red light flashed and the cameras began to roll, and suddenly he was speaking live to the nation.

She watched on the screen, so that she could read the English subtitles, and much of it she missed, because her heart was beating so fast with nerves and excitement and protectiveness.

But key phrases would stay in her mind and her heart for ever.

'I have been charged with the running of our coun-

try.' His face grew very serious at this point. *'An awesome responsibility which I have always embraced and cherished. But your Ruler must be allowed to fulfil his own personal destiny in order to best discharge his duties to his homeland.'*

He sent her the briefest of looks before continuing. *'In Qudamah, your Sheikh is permitted by law to have a harem of up to sixty women.'*

Sienna sat bolt upright. She hadn't known *that*!

'But I do not wish to have sixty women. I wish for only one, for I believe in monogamy.'

There was an unmistakable ripple in the room—as if he had just come out and declared that he had converted to cannibalism!

Now his eyes were on her, and they were very steady.

'For I have found my very own houri, and I intend to make her my wife.'

Later, Sienna would discover the significance of that particular word. A houri was a beautiful young woman but—far more crucially—she was a *virgin*. He was telling his people that he had found a bride who, although she might not at first appear so, was actually a suitable bride for their Sheikh.

She would also learn that Abdul-Aziz had travelled to England with the intention of attempting to bribe her with unimaginable riches to stay away from the Sheikh. But then he had seen her playing with Cara in the homespun tranquillity of her mother's house.

'I realised that I had never allowed myself to think beyond the stereotype of what I believed you to be,' he told her. 'And of course by then I realised that my Sheikh had grown to love you—and suddenly I could see why.'

And it didn't take long to realise that Hashim's mother wanted only her son's happiness.

For when it all came down to it palaces and different cultures counted for very little. In the end, the human spirit was the same the world over.

EPILOGUE

A DOLLOP of mashed banana landed in a slimy lump on the back of her hand and Sienna giggled as she wiped it away, looking up into the bemused black eyes of her husband as he surveyed the breakfast scene before him.

Hashim smiled. How his life had been transformed! Gone was the starchy formality and the slow glide of numerous servants who catered to his every whim. Instead, there sat his beautiful Sienna, with their gorgeous wriggling son on her lap.

'What a merry dance he leads you,' he observed ruefully.

'Ah, but what wonderful co-ordination he has,' cooed Sienna. 'Only eight months old, and he's practically feeding himself!'

'Indeed,' he murmured diplomatically, as another dollop of fruit was relayed across the linen table-cloth by the lively Prince Marzug.

Hashim had long given up trying to get Sienna to bring their son up in the conventional manner of royal princes, and she had resolutely refused to have child-care except when strictly necessary.

'No one can love a baby like his mother,' she had

told him firmly. 'Or his father,' she had added impishly.

And in that he could not argue with her—though he enjoyed trying. For Marzug had stolen his heart the moment he had made his first lusty bawl. There was so much love in Hashim's world now. His senses were raw and on fire with it. And Sienna had started it all. He looked at her.

Hard to believe as she sat in this scene of cosy domesticity, despite the grand dimensions of the room, that last night she had stunned the visiting French Ambassador at a reception given at the Palace in his honour. Hashim had watched with pride and love and lust as she had danced—slender and graceful as a flower swayed by the summer breeze. And alone afterwards, in the glorious privacy of their apartment, she had…she had… Hashim swallowed.

'Are you all right, darling?' Sienna questioned innocently, her words cutting in to a train of thought which was probably not advisable when he was due to inspect the Qudamah army in a little under an hour.

'Yes, my beauty,' he murmured, watching her pick up a cream sheet of paper. 'What are you reading now?'

Absently, Sienna dropped a kiss onto Marzug's curly black hair. 'Oh, just a request—asking if I will be patron of the new children's charity which is being set up in Nasim.'

'*Another* charity?' Hashim frowned. 'But you do enough already.'

'I know. But some of the work is extra-special, and…' She put the letter down on the table, out of Marzug's reach, and smiled at him. 'I'm just flattered to be asked,' she said simply.

And he understood. Perfectly.

Because it hadn't been all plain sailing to get to where she was today. Sienna had had to work hard to get the people of Qudamah to accept her. Some of them hadn't—certainly not straight away—but she had understood their doubts and fears about their beloved Sheikh marrying a woman from so far away, who knew little of their culture.

And there were some who had not finally thawed until she had produced the plump and bouncing olive-skinned infant Prince and fireworks had lit up the skies behind the Palace. Then they had finally taken her into their hearts.

The wedding itself had been a bit of a challenge, too—there had been a civil ceremony and then a religious one, after her conversion to Hashim's faith. She'd had to memorise all her vows in Qudamahesh and she had spent the night before the marriage saying them over and over again, until she was word perfect. Learning the ancient language was something she had immediately set about doing—and was even more of a challenge!

But she was young and bright and eager to learn. And she was in love. Just as she was loved. And that put everything in its proper perspective.

She had been a bag of nerves before her first meet-

ing with Hashim's mother—for the Princess was
deeply revered by all who knew her. But their shared
love for one man had been enough to unite them in
a harmony which had soon grown into genuine re-
gard.

She was both a wise and a perceptive woman. She
had allayed some of Sienna's fears—recounting the
tale of one of Hashim's ancestors, who had married
the daughter of his fiercest enemy despite much opposition. 'So, you see, there is nothing new under the
sun, Sienna,' she had said softly. 'No matter where
they live, nor what they do, people are the same; they
never change. They fall in love and they fight for that
love, and that is just how it should be.'

Sienna knew that what Hashim's mother had told
her was important. Not to compare, no—but to realise
that life was very precious and very short. Once, she
had wondered when the present became the past, but
now she realised that it was happening all the time.
Their wedding was already in the past, and their life
would whizz by as everyone warned it did. They just
had to make the most of it.

She pushed the bowl of banana away and Hashim
judged it safe enough to reach out and ruffle his son's
hair. 'Will we swim together later?' she questioned
eagerly. 'In the Palace pool? Just the three of us?'

'Yes, my love,' Hashim murmured indulgently,
wondering what the fabled Special Guard of the army
might say if they could see their Commander-in-Chief
being such putty in his wife's hands! 'And later we

will have dinner alone.' His eyes glinted. 'Since our diaries are free. And at some point we must discuss your mother's visit, and the gift of the stallion I intend to make to her.'

'Oh, Hashim, she's going to be over the moon.'

He took her hand, briefly rubbing the shiny gold wedding band with the pad of his thumb and then lifting her fingers to his lips, licking them provocatively. His eyes captured hers with sensual allure. 'Well, then,' he said lightly. 'That makes two of us, doesn't it?'

'Three of us, actually.' She smiled. 'Well, four if you count Marzug.'

'Always.'

Their eyes met and Sienna's breath caught in her throat. She wanted to hold that moment in her heart for ever.

She had to remember that it didn't last long—and to say the things that counted.

'I love you, Hashim.'

His eyes were tender. 'I love you too, sweet Sienna.'

And Sienna put the baby in his highchair and moved into her husband's arms, wrapping herself close enough to feel the powerful beating of his heart.

MILLS & BOON®

Live the emotion

Modern
romance™

SALE OR RETURN BRIDE *by Sarah Morgan*

Sebastien Fiorukis is to marry Alesia Philipos. Their families have been feuding for generations, but it seems finally the rift is healed. However, all is not as it seems. Alesia has been bought by her husband – and she will *not* be a willing wife!

PRINCE'S PASSION *by Carole Mortimer*

Award-winning director Nik Prince is bent on transforming a bestseller into a movie – but he must find the author. Jinx Nixon knows the identity of the writer, but she won't reveal it! But Nik's sizzling good looks mean she must fight to control the fierce attraction she feels for him…

THE MANCINI MARRIAGE BARGAIN *by Trish Morey*

Paolo Mancini married Helene Grainger to save her from a forced marriage – twelve years on he's back, to tell her they can divorce. But Paolo is still the gorgeous Italian Helene married, and when they are reunited he realises he has no intention of letting his wife go…

THE RICH MAN'S VIRGIN *by Lindsay Armstrong*

Millionaire Jack McKinnon got virginal Maggie pregnant and he wants to marry her. Maggie has fought for independence, and she isn't about to let her life be taken over by this man. But it's one thing to take a stand for herself – it's quite another when she's carrying Jack's baby…

breast cancer CAMPAIGN

researching the cure

The facts you need to know:

- **One woman in nine** in the United Kingdom will develop breast cancer during her lifetime.

- Each year **40,700** women are newly diagnosed with breast cancer and around **12,800** women will die from the disease. However, survival rates are improving, with on average 77 per cent of women still alive five years later.

- **Men can also suffer from breast cancer**, although currently they make up less than one per cent of all new cases of the disease.

Britain has one of the highest breast cancer death rates in the world. Breast Cancer Campaign wants to understand why and do something about it. Statistics cannot begin to describe the impact that breast cancer has on the lives of those women who are affected by it and on their families and friends.

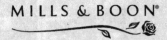

MILLS & BOON®

**During the month of October
Harlequin Mills & Boon will donate
10p from the sale of every
Modern Romance™ series book to
help Breast Cancer Campaign
in *researching the cure*.**

Breast Cancer Campaign's scientific projects
look at improving diagnosis and treatment
of breast cancer, better understanding how
it develops and ultimately either curing the
disease or preventing it.

Do your part to help

Visit <u>www.breastcancercampaign.org</u>

And make a donation today.

researching the cure

Breast Cancer Campaign is a company limited by guarantee registered in England and
Wales. Company No. 05074725. Charity registration No. 299758.

FREE!

4 Books
and a surprise gift!

We would like to take this opportunity to thank you for reading this Mills & Boon® book by offering you the chance to take FOUR more specially selected titles from the Modern Romance™ series absolutely FREE! We're also making this offer to introduce you to the benefits of the Reader Service™—

- ★ **FREE home delivery**
- ★ **FREE gifts and competitions**
- ★ **FREE monthly Newsletter**
- ★ **Exclusive Reader Service offers**
- ★ **Books available before they're in the shops**

Accepting these FREE books and gift places you under no obligation to buy, you may cancel at any time, even after receiving your free shipment. Simply complete your details below and return the entire page to the address below. You don't even need a stamp!

YES! Please send me 4 free Modern Romance books and a surprise gift. I understand that unless you hear from me, I will receive 6 superb new titles every month for just £2.75 each, postage and packing free. I am under no obligation to purchase any books and may cancel my subscription at any time. The free books and gift will be mine to keep in any case.

P5ZEF

Ms/Mrs/Miss/Mr .... Initials ....

BLOCK CAPITALS PLEASE

Surname ....

Address..

....

....Postcode ....

Send this whole page to:
UK: FREEPOST CN81, Croydon, CR9 3WZ